Contents

KV-011-967

Wee, sleekit, cow'rin tim'rous beastie.

14,600 Scottish books
Over 160 author biographies
Over 30 author interviews
Updated daily

BooksfromScotland.com

Introduction

The *Directory of Publishing in Scotland* is now in its seventeenth edition. It was first produced in 1988 in response to the many daily queries received from the press, the public and other organisations. The publishing industry has undergone massive change since then with a proliferation of new technologies, not least email and web, but the printed format of the directory remains perennially popular for all those seeking publishers, resources, information and business contacts.

The *Yearbook* provides information on Scottish publishers and individuals and companies who service the industry's needs, such as agents, designers, indexers, editors and printers. There are also lists of booksellers, libraries, publishing training providers, relevant literary and other organisations and resources.

We would like to extend our thanks to the individuals, companies and organisations listed for their support, and also to the readers and users who have contributed comments and suggestions for this edition.

Finally, and most importantly, we would like to thank Matthew Thomson and Thomson Litho Ltd for their continuing and much appreciated support of this publication.

Publishing Industry

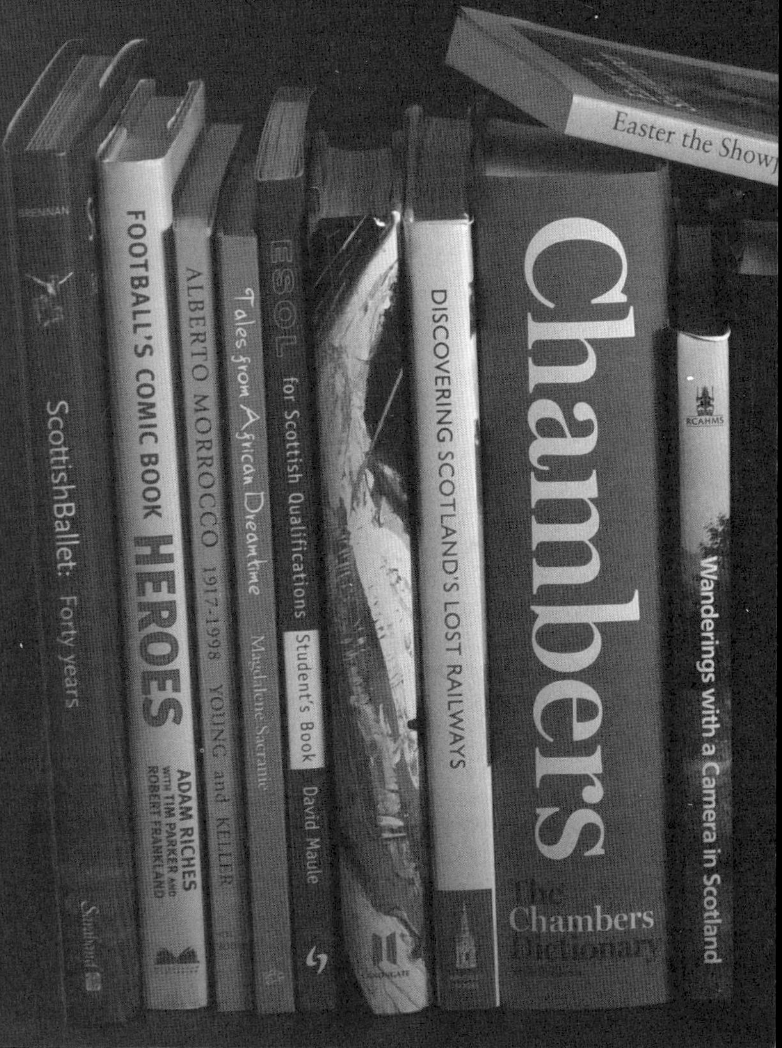

The Publishing Industry In Scotland

Publishing in Scotland

Marion Sinclair, Chief Executive, Publishing Scotland

Publishing is one of the world's foremost creative industries. From the genesis of an idea in the mind of the writer or editor to the producing of the book by the editorial, design, production, and marketing teams, the decisions made have to be both innovative and commercially viable. If the book captures the public imagination, then it can lead to bestseller status, to a film, TV series, computer games and merchandising spin-offs. Many, of course, do not, but are no less important for that.

The book remains at the heart of entertainment and leisure pursuits (to say nothing of its value to the world of education, literacy and research) and, surprisingly, is the single biggest media product in the UK in terms of sales, outstripping DVDs, games, newspapers etc.

The industry is undergoing huge transformation, in common with other media. Digital technology is evolving at such a rapid pace that it is difficult to keep up with all the new products and services on offer. In publishing as in music, photography, home computing, and mobile communications, it can seem as if all the emphasis is on downloads, storing information, file sharing, and other methods of delivery. Publishing is, however, much more than delivery, and the acquiring of good stories and content remains at the heart of the industry.

Today's publishers need to be able to think simultaneously of the writer, the book, the formats, the production, sales channels, and the retail environment: a complex mix of people and processes that requires instinct, agility, business acumen, forecasting skills, and an increasingly sure grasp of technical knowledge. Large conglomerates and companies employ people with those skills spread throughout the workforce. Small and medium companies often have to outsource to gain those skills, and if very small, they multitask, but there is only one game in the end – that of getting your content across to the readers – and in order to play, publishers need to keep match-fit.

For many publishers, the domestic market remains their prime focus and source of titles and revenue. Those publishers who do operate internationally and regularly feature more international titles do well in export markets.

In 2010 we await the birth of a new body, Creative Scotland, the proposed successor to the Scottish Arts Council and Scottish Screen. With its stated aim of making 'Scotland a place where more creative people choose to work and live' it is to be hoped that the support for the arts and creative industries will be enhanced. The fact that Scottish publishers live next door to one of the most powerful publishing countries in the world still represents significant challenges. The need for greater professionalisation, skills, business development, and investment within the industry is an aspect that Publishing Scotland continues to address in the coming year, to accompany the support of publishing as a cultural activity.

We're also there for training, information seminars, networking, co-operative initiatives, hosting stands at book fairs, technology updates, and lobbying on policy matters to government agencies. We also supply distribution services via BookSource in Glasgow and an online information site, BooksfromScotland.com. Now in our 36th year with a current membership of 110 companies and individuals, Publishing Scotland aims to support and build capacity across the range of companies in Scotland, most of whom fall into the small and medium-size company bracket.

Some vital statistics about publishing in Scotland: about 110 book publishing companies based all over Scotland, from Shetland to the Borders, sell their books to a worldwide market. Publishers in Scotland produce around 2,000 new titles each year. Publishing is done across virtually all genres: fiction, academic, educational, professional, scientific, children's, reference, biography, travel, history etc. Around 1,250 people are employed directly by the industry, plus freelance workers such as many of our network members – agents, editors, designers, authors, printers and illustrators – all contributing to the spectrum of creative talent and feeding their services into the industry. The book and journal publishing activity in Scotland generates an estimated £343 million and ranges from HarperCollins to one-person start-ups. The barriers to entry in the industry are few but competition for retail space and review coverage is extremely fierce.

MEMBER HIGHLIGHTS

Canongate Books won Publisher of the Year 2009 at the British Book Industry Awards.

Some of our publisher members' books that won prizes and awards during the past year:

· **Barrington Stoke's** 101 Ways to Get Your Child to Read by Patience Thomson won the Quick Reads Learners' Favourite Award

· Barack Obama's bestseller for **Canongate**, Dreams from My Father, won the Galaxy British Book Awards Biography of the Year 2009

· **Canongate's** Booker-prize winner The Life of Pi won the British Book Design and Production award for the Limited Edition and Fine Binding category

· **Edinburgh University Press's** A History Of Scottish Philosophy: Alexander Broadie won the 2009 Saltire Society History Book of the Year

· **Floris Books'** *First Aid for Fairies and Other Fabled Beasts* by Lari Don won the 2009 Royal Mail Children's Book Award in the Younger Readers category

· **Mainstream Publishing's** *When Friday Comes: Football in the War Zone* by James Montague won Best New Writer at the British Sports Books Awards

· **Mainstream Publishing's** *Seeing Red: Twelve Tumultuous Years in Welsh Rugby* by Alun Carter and Nick Bishop won Best Rugby Book at the British Sports Books Awards

Publishing Scotland

ABOUT PUBLISHING SCOTLAND

In April 2007 Publishing Scotland reformed itself into a new organisation. Known as the Scottish Publishers Association for over thirty years, the new name reflects a wider remit and membership, better placed to pick up on new directions and trends as they emerge.

The body aims to support work across the whole spectrum of the publishing sector in Scotland, as a key part of the Creative Industries, through its range of services, training, information provision, development of infrastructure, and book fair representation.

The remit of the organisation has always included a cultural role: our task is to ensure that publishers in Scotland are best placed to pick up on, develop and nurture new talent and to develop an infrastructure to reach audiences.

Publishing Scotland has a newly constituted board that offers a depth of experience in publishing to complement the management team and the reorganised Publishers' Advisory Committee.

The new category of membership, that of the 'network member' has added a further dimension in widening the criteria beyond print-based publishers to designers, literary agents, editors and, particularly, to the Society of Authors in Scotland.

There is no other body representing the content providers in the book publishing sector in Scotland and we aim to play our part in ensuring that there is a vibrant publishing sector - vital in order to give writers a start, a showcase for their talents, and a route to audiences. Small creative companies can access generic business advice and support from other quarters but the specifics of the books sector can only be handled by a body that can call upon an extensive range of contacts and experience.

There are obvious and essential links with the literature sector in Scotland; we see our work as complementary to the work on literacy, writer support, literature promotion, and outreach undertaken by other bodies.

We plan to develop services in the period 2010–11, to build on past work that will deliver a strong, capable and vibrant industry, to serve the needs of the writers and their audiences. The sector, like most other creative sectors these days, is going through rapid changes in terms of reading habits, formats, and digital, technological change. Keeping viable the outlets for creative work will be a challenge but one which we fully intend to respond to.

VISION, AIMS AND OBJECTIVES
Vision

To become the lead body for the Publishing sector in Scotland by supporting and helping create an environment that allows publishers, writers and content producers to innovate; and to play a part in fostering excellence in the production and delivery of creative content in the 21st century.

Aims
- To develop and promote the work of companies in the Publishing sector to an international audience
- To run a first-class skills and training programme for the sector
- To develop a comprehensive network of publishers, content creators and service providers to allow access to key markets, information, and opportunities
- To gather information, to survey, and to research the needs of the sector
- To act as the voice of the sector

Publishing Scotland's objectives
1. To develop the capabilities and competences of existing publishing companies by engaging in a programme of joint initiatives and skills enhancement, and in facilitating new ways of delivering cultural and other content to new audiences
2. To increase the number of training courses and widen their scope to include new ways of delivering content, digitisation, and new technology
3. To develop a network of publishers, content creators and service providers involving a seminar programme, new events, and information provision
4. To establish a data gathering survey that will provide valuable statistics on the scope, range, and opportunities within the sector and allow analysis of trends in the sector
5. To represent the sector at all appropriate fora, from Creative Industry sector involvement to specific publishing and literature groups
6. To enhance the infrastructure and resources for the Publishing sector by developing the work of BookSource and BooksfromScotland.com

MEMBERSHIP

There are at present two categories of membership of Publishing Scotland – publisher and network.

Publisher membership is open to all book and print-based publishers or online and electronic publishers (including digital publishers). Companies must be based in Scotland or publish predominantly Scottish material. Membership is also open to content providers, packagers and organisations or institutions who produce or trade in books or intellectual property. Please see our website for a list of the publisher membership criteria.

Network membership is open to those individuals and companies who work with or within the publishing industry but who do not publish. It is also open to non-publishing libraries. Current network members include illustrators, designers, literary agents, editors, translators, print and digitisation companies, authors (through the Society of Authors in Scotland membership) and universities. Network members must be based in Scotland, supply goods and/or services to publishers, have training and expertise and work professionally within the publishing sector.

Services to members

Publisher members benefit from an annual programme of activities which offer opportunities to all publishers, whatever their size, scope, speciality or geographical location. These activities are organised on a cooperative basis in order to save costs and administrative time. They include attendance at book fairs (home and abroad); marketing to bookshops, schools and libraries; publicity and advertising services; catalogue mailings and website information; provision of professional training in publishing skills; information resources and business advice. We also work on liaison with the UK bookchains. In addition, Publishing Scotland implements research, develops projects and liaises with outside organisations which are considered to be of interest and benefit to the membership of Publishing Scotland, for example with the Publishing Training Centre, universities, the British Council, the Scottish Government and Scottish Enterprise.

BOOKSFROMSCOTLAND.COM

BooksfromScotland.com offers an online shop-front designed specifically to feature, promote and sell Scottish-interest books. Our comprehensive list of over 14,500 books includes:
- Scottish authors – from Alexander McCall Smith to Walter Scott to Ian Rankin
- Scottish subjects – history, travel guides, biographies
- Scottish publishers – books published by a Scottish company, including all Publishing Scotland members

The information-rich site offers a wealth of news and events listings, author profiles and interviews, articles and features, and is updated daily.

Publishers will be interested in our popular Publisher of the Month feature, a free way to highlight a publisher's backlist and forthcoming titles, or to launch a new imprint or list.

Individual titles can be featured as a Book of the Month or a Children's Book of the Month – a high-profile feature on our website homepage and in our monthly emails which are sent to readers interested in Scottish writing the world over.

To make the most of BooksfromScotland.com, publishers can submit enhanced title information – better cover blurbs, tables of contents, extracts and sample chapters. Submit authors to be interviewed or to be featured as an Author of the Month. Send in information about launch events and author signings. Ask your authors to blog for BooksfromScotland.com. There are lots of ways in which the website can help promote your books.

TRAINING
All members of Publishing Scotland are also able to take advantage of training courses and seminars on a wide range of publishing issues at reduced member rates (these are also available to non-members for a higher fee). See our website (www.publishingscotland.org/publishingtraining) for an up-to-date listing.

FINANCING PUBLISHING SCOTLAND
Financial assistance comes from the Scottish Arts Council, subscriptions paid by members, and charges made for services.

HOW PUBLISHING SCOTLAND IS GOVERNED
Publishing Scotland's Board
Publishing Scotland is governed by a Board which is made up of five publisher members, two network members, Publishing Scotland CEO and up to four non-executive members. The current Board consists of:

Keith Whittles, Whittles Publishing (Chair)
Angus Konstam, author (Vice-Chair)
Christian Maclean, Floris Books (Treasurer)
Caroline Gorham, Canongate Books
Mike Miller, Geddes & Grosset
Ann Crawford, Saint Andrew Press
Kathleen Brown, Triwords Ltd
Marion Sinclair, CEO, Publishing Scotland
Simon Brown, Anderson Strathern
Ernst Kallus, North Plains
Anthony Kinahan, Dunedin Academic Press

Publishers' Advisory Committee

Reporting to the Board is the Publishers' Advisory Committee (PAC). This committee is made up of member publishers and deals with issues specifically relating to the publishers, for instance, cooperative marketing, bookfairs, information and advice. The PAC currently consists of:

Ann Crawford, Saint Andrew Press (Chair)
Christian Maclean, Floris Books
Mike Miller, Geddes & Grosset
John Mitchell, Hodder Gibson
Neil Wilson, Neil Wilson Publishing
Anthony Kinahan, Dunedin Academic Press
Sonia Raphael, Barrington Stoke Ltd
Keith Charters, Strident Publishing
Sarah Falconer, Leckie & Leckie
Sarah Mitchell, Bright Red Publishing
Richard Hallewell, Hallewell Publishing

CONTACT PUBLISHING SCOTLAND

Address: Scottish Book Centre, 137 Dundee St, Edinburgh EH11 1BG
Tel: 0131 228 6866
Fax: 0131 228 3220
Email: firstname.lastname@publishingscotland.org
Website: www.publishingscotland.org
Date established: 1973 (as Scottish Publishers Association)
Contacts: Marion Sinclair, CEO; Jane Walker, Member Services; Joan Lyle, Information and Training; Lorraine Fenton, Finance and Administration; Liam Davison, BooksfromScotland.com.

Services offered: training, events and seminars, information and support, networking, trade fair support, lobbying, trade liaison, distribution (through BookSource), online bookselling and promotion (through BooksfromScotland.com)

Publishing Scotland Publisher Members

Features and Benefits of Publisher Membership

Strong representation on the key issues, nationally and internationally, is the principal benefit of joining Publishing Scotland. Publisher members benefit from an annual programme of activities which offer opportunities to all publishers, whatever their size, scope, speciality or geographical location. Many of our services are included as part of the subscription fee; the services that we do charge for are marked with a * below. We endeavour to keep our costs for our fee-paying services as low as possible.

TRADE
- Publisher contacts with major UK bookshops, online retailers, Visit Scotland, Historic Scotland and the National Trust for Scotland through the UK Trade Committee
- Face-to-face events with booksellers, eg meetings between members and Waterstone's, Amazon and Independent Booksellers
- Distribution services through BookSource *
- Industry Data

TRAINING AND SKILLS DEVELOPMENT
- Tailored, subsidised training courses on a wide range of publishing skills, including proofreading, writing for the web and book design *
- Bespoke courses for your company through our network of highly specialised and experienced industry experts and trainers *
- Seminars on all aspects of publishing
- Opportunity to serve on the Publishing Scotland Board and participation on various committees and working parties

BOOK FAIRS
- Hire display and meeting space on our *Publishers from Scotland* collective stands at London and Frankfurt Book Fairs and BookExpo America *
- All members (even if they are not attending) may send catalogues to London and Frankfurt Book Fairs for distribution from our collective stand
- Display and sell your titles in the largest selection of Scottish books in the UK annually at the Edinburgh International Book Festival *

MARKETING
- An entry in the *Publishing Scotland Yearbook* and a copy of the *Yearbook*
- Library partnership initiatives
- Presence on the Publishing Scotland website – including advertising of your vacancies and events
- Books from Scotland.com – including Publisher of the Month

- There are further opportunities to market your titles through BooksfromScotland.com for a fee, such as Book of the Month or a seasonal advertising campaign *
- Mailings and co-operative marketing opportunities *

INFORMATION

- Regular email bulletin on the latest and newest updates on UK Trade, events, seminars, business advice and also includes latest vacancies
- Information and advice from Publishing Scotland's staff members and access to our comprehensive industry library
- Publishing Scotland annual conference *
- AGM
- Exclusive members area on our website

SOCIAL

- Christmas and Summer members' social events
- Hire of our premises *

List of Publisher Members

The publishers listed on pages 19–81 are all members of Publishing Scotland. Some, like Canongate, were founder members of Publishing Scotland' predecessor the SPA in 1973, others joined as soon as they started up like Mainstream Publishing in 1978. Many others are long-time and committed members making valuable contributions to the organisation as well as to the publishing industry in Scotland.

Over time new publishers start up, existing publishers merge or are taken over, owners reorganise leading to revitalisation or sometimes to departure of well-known names. The publishing industry is constantly changing and our current list reflects that. As we go to press in December 2009, we are pleased to welcome several new members: Academy Media, Grace Note Publishing, Serafina Press, Vagabond Voices and Witherby Seamanship International. Covering a wide range of publications (Scots and Gaelic, Illustrated Children's, translated works and marine), they also cover the country (from the Isle of Lewis to Eyemouth, via Crieff and Livingston) and range from a sole publisher to one of the largest independent publishing companies in Scotland.

It is impossible to know how many publishers there are in Scotland (many individuals and companies publish only occasionally or as part of another main business), but we are confident that because of its members, Publishing Scotland is the body that best represents and speaks for the publishing industry in Scotland.

ACADEMY MEDIA PS

For over thirty years we have been making programmes about history, literature, music and languages. By introducing a few of the great writers and composers of recent centuries through our video biographies we hope to unlock some of
the world's artistic treasures which will help people to grapple more readily with
the past! Our current list includes:

Famous authors: Austen, Blake, Brontë, Burns, Confucius, Defoe, Dickens,
Dickinson, George Eliot, Faulkner, Fitzgerald, Goethe, Hardy, Hemingway,
Hugo, Ibsen, James, Johnson, Joyce, Kafka, Keats, Lawrence, Melville, O'Neill,
Orwell, Poe, Proust, Scott, Shakespeare, Shaw, Shelley, Steinbeck, Stevenson,
Swift, Twain, Voltaire, Whitman, Wilde, Woolf, Wordsworth, Yeats, Zola

Famous composers: Bach, Beethoven, Brahms, Chopin, Handel, Haydn, Mozart,
Puccini, Ravel, Schubert, Sibelius, Richard Strauss, Stravinsky, Tchaikovsky,
Verdi, Wagner

History & society: *Have You Seen The Parthenon?*, *King Rama VI of Thailand, Bangkok,
The Divine City*, *A History of China* (5-disc series to be released December 2009)

Classic dramas: Ibsen's *Ghosts* (Full-length feature released 2007)

Languages: *Visite en France I & II* (Intermediate French conversation programmes
with accompanying texts)

CONTACTS
Address: Academy Media, Firth View, Gower Street, Brora KW9 6PU
Tel: 01408 622 183
Email: info@academymedia.com
Website: www.academymedia.com

ACAIR PS

Acair publishes a variety of texts and is the principal publisher of Gaelic texts for children in Scotland.

Established in 1978 the company has up to 1,000 titles to its credit. We have strong links with English publishers, joining them in co-editions, sometimes publishing up to 15 such titles in a year.

We work closely with children's Gaelic authors and translators to also produce original Gaelic texts for children and with the National Gaelic Curriculum Service to produce material suitable for use in Gaelic medium education.

Our adult Gaelic publications include texts by renowned Gaelic poets such as Sorley MacLean, Donald MacAulay, Derick Thomson, Angus Peter Campbell and Christopher Whyte, often accompanied by parallel English translations, as well as photographic journals of island historical contexts both past and present.

Acair books have won literature prizes over the years at the Royal National Mod as well as accolades for design and presentation.

Established: 1977
Publications (yearly average): 10 per year
Types of books published: Children's Gaelic, historical in Gaelic and English, poetry, plays, music, photographic, biography, environmental studies, Gaelic language
Submission details: Submissions welcome

CONTACTS
People: Norma Macleod (Manager/Editor); Margaret Anne Macleod (Design); Margaret Martin (Administration); Donalda Riddell (Stock Control & Marketing)
Address: 7 James Street, Stornoway, Isle of Lewis HS1 2QN
Tel: 01851 703 020
Fax: 01851 703 294
Email: info@acairbooks.com
Website: www.acairbooks.com
Distributor: BookSource, 50 Cambuslang Road, Cambuslang, Glasgow G32 8NB; Tel: 0845 370 0067; Fax: 0845 370 0068

ASSOCIATION FOR SCOTTISH LITERARY STUDIES PS

Part-funded by the Scottish Arts Council, ASLS publishes classic works of Scottish literature; essays, monographs and journals on the literature and languages of Scotland; and *Scotnotes*, a series of study guides to major Scottish writers. We also produce *New Writing Scotland*, an annual anthology of contemporary poetry and prose in English, Gaelic and Scots. Online publications include the *International Journal of Scottish Literature* (www.ijsl.stir.ac.uk) and the ezine *The Bottle Imp* (www.thebottleimp.org.uk).

Each year, ASLS holds annual conferences on Scottish writers in such diverse locations as Glasgow, Kirkwall, Edinburgh and Skye. Other annual conferences address Scottish language issues, and the place of Scottish literature and language in the classroom. Our schools conferences are suitable for CPD (Continuous Professional Development), and attract teachers from across Scotland.

Along with other Scottish literary organisations and the SAC, ASLS campaigns for a greater appreciation, both at home and abroad, in schools, colleges and universities, of Scotland's literary culture.

Established: 1970
Publications (yearly average): 12
Types of books published: Works of Scottish literature which have been neglected; anthologies of new Scottish writing in English, Gaelic and Scots; essays and monographs on the literature and languages of Scotland; comprehensive study guides to major Scottish writers. ASLS membership is open to all. In 2010, a subscription of £40.00 (individuals) or £67.00 (corporate) buys: one Annual Volume; *New Writing Scotland*; *Scottish Literary Review* (2 issues); *ScotLit* (2 issues); *Scottish Language* (1 issue). Special packages for schools and students are also available.
Submission details: Submissions are invited to *New Writing Scotland*. Please see the ASLS website for detailed submission instructions.

CONTACTS
People: Duncan Jones (General Manager)
Address: Department of Scottish Literature, University of Glasgow, 7 University Gardens, Glasgow G12 8QH
Tel/fax: 0141 330 5309
Email: office@asls.org.uk
Website: www.asls.org.uk
Distributor: BookSource, 50 Cambuslang Road, Cambuslang, Glasgow G32 8NB; Tel: 0845 370 0067; Fax: 0845 370 0068

BOURNE

ATELIER BOOKS 🅿🆂

Atelier Books, the publishing imprint of Bourne Fine Art, was launched in 1991. Atelier publishes monographs on Scottish artists. Whilst all titles are available to view and buy at Bourne Fine Art, orders are not taken. If you wish to place an order please contact our distributor, BookSource, direct.

Established: 1987
Publications (yearly average): Variable
Types of books published: Books on art and artists

CONTACTS
People: Athina Athanasiadou
Address: 6 Dundas Street, Edinburgh EH3 6HZ
Tel: 0131 557 4050
Fax: 0131 557 8382
Email: art@bournefineart.com
Website: www.bournefineart.com
Distributor: BookSource, 50 Cambuslang Road, Cambuslang, Glasgow G32 8NB; Tel: 0845 370 0067; Fax: 0845 370 0068

BARRINGTON STOKE LTD PS

Barrington Stoke publish accessible, enjoyable and unpatronising short books for children who are dyslexic, struggling to read, or simply reluctant to sit down with a book.

We offer great stories by some of the best children's authors working today. Each book is read before publication by struggling readers of the right age and reading ability, so that we know the final book is a terrific and accessible read. And, there's nothing on the up-to-the-minute covers to suggest that the books are for less fluent readers.

Winner of the Lightning Source Children's Publisher of the Year (Independent Publishing Awards 2007), Barrington Stoke has had books selected for Booktrust's 2007 and 2008 Booked Up programmes, and is publishing 101 *Ways to Get Your Child to Read* as part of the nationwide Quick Reads publishing programme for World Book Day 2009.

Established: 1997
Publications (yearly average): 70
Types of books published: Fiction, non-fiction and plays from award-winning authors for dyslexic, struggling and reluctant readers between the ages of 8 and 16, with a reading age of 7 or 8. Books for seriously struggling readers with a reading age of 6 (Go!). Fiction for adults with a reading age of 8 (Most Wanted). Also teacher, parent and learning resources.
Submission details: Do not accept unsolicited manuscripts

CONTACTS
People: Sonia Raphael (Managing Director)
Address: 18 Walker Street, Edinburgh EH3 7LP
Tel (general): 0131 225 4113
Tel (schools enquiries): 0131 225 4213
Fax: 0131 225 4140
Email (general): info@barringtonstoke.co.uk
Email (schools enquiries): schools@barringtonstoke.co.uk
Website: www.barringtonstoke.co.uk
Distributor: Macmillan Distribution Ltd, Brunel Road, Houndmills, Basingstoke, Hampshire RG21 6XS; Tel: 01256 329 242; Fax: 01256 812 521/558; Email: mdl@macmillan.co.uk

BLACK & WHITE PUBLISHING [PS]

Since 1999, Black & White Publishing has produced a wide range of titles with over 250 now in print, including 30 in the award-winning Itchy Coo imprint of children's books in the Scots language as well as the B&W classics list. We publish an extensive range of titles including general non-fiction, biography, sport and humour, as well as selected fiction and children's books.

Established: 1999
Publications (yearly average): 40–50
Types of books published: General non-fiction; memoirs; biographies; sport; true crime; cookery; humour; fiction; Scottish literature
Submission details: Please send a brief synopsis along with 30 sample pages. Please do **not** submit full manuscripts. Submission by email preferred. Email address: mail@blackandwhitepublishing.com. For full submission guidelines, please look at our website www.blackandwhitepublishing.com.

CONTACTS
People: Campbell Brown (Managing Director); Alison McBride (Marketing Director); John Richardson (Production Manager); Janne Moller (Rights); Rachel Kuck (Production and Administration)
Address: 29 Ocean Drive, Leith, Edinburgh EH6 6JL
Tel: 0131 625 4500
Fax: 0131 625 4501
Email: mail@blackandwhitepublishing.com
Website: www.blackandwhitepublishing.com
Distributor: BookSource, 50 Cambuslang Road, Cambuslang, Glasgow G32 8NB; Tel: 0845 370 0067; Fax: 0845 370 0068

BRIGHT RED PUBLISHING PS

Bright Red Publishing was founded in 2008 as a completely independent Scottish educational publishing company, and by the start of 2009 had become the new publisher of the Official SQA Past Papers.

As well as the Past Papers, we produce other accessible, contemporary and engaging materials for Scotland's students and teachers, for which we are already gaining a strong reputation for quality.

One of the ways we achieve this quality is to work with the very best publishing and educational professionals in Scotland. We aim to be a positive and self-sustaining publishing company, and we value the people we work with and the relationships we build in the course of our business.

Bright Red books are developed to be fresh, bright, comprehensive and easy to use, so that they will inspire young minds to think creatively and achieve their full potential.

Established: 2008
Publications (yearly average): 100
Types of books published: Official SQA Past Papers with Answers; revision, exam preparation and teaching and learning materials for the Scottish curriculum

CONTACTS
People: Richard Bass; Alan Grierson; John MacPherson; Sarah Mitchell
Address: 6 Stafford Street, Edinburgh EH3 7AU
Tel: 0131 220 5804
Fax: 0131 220 6710
Email: info@brightredpublishing.co.uk
Website: www.brightredpublishing.co.uk
Distributor: Bright Red Publishing Ltd

BROWN & WHITTAKER PUBLISHING PS

Brown & Whittaker specialise in books about the Isle of Mull - our books about walking, local history, archaeology, genealogy and wildlife are recognised as being accurate and up to date.

Established: 1985
Publications (yearly average): 2
Types of books published: Isle of Mull, history, archaeology, wildlife, genealogy, walking guides
Submission details: Anything relevant to Mull considered, but not children's books

CONTACTS
People: Olive Brown and Jean Whittaker
Address: Tobermory, Isle of Mull PA75 6PR
Tel: 01688 302 381/302 171
Fax: 01688 302 140
Email: olivebrown@msn.com
Website: www.brown-whittaker.co.uk
Distributor: Brown & Whittaker Publishing

BROWN, SON & FERGUSON, LTD PS

We were established around 1850 and publish around 7 books per annum. We mainly publish nautical and some yachting publications. Our main publication is *Brown's Nautical Almanac* which is published annually, also *The Nautical Magazine*, published monthly, technical and non-technical publications, ships' stationery, model ship building and one-act and full length plays.

Established: c 1850

CONTACTS
People: Nigel Brown (Managing Director), Steven Readings (Sales Manager)
Address: 4–10 Darnley Street, Glasgow G41 2SD
Tel: 0141 429 1234
Fax: 0141 420 1694
Email: info@skipper.co.uk
Website: www.skipper.co.uk
Distributor: Brown, Son & Ferguson, Ltd

CANONGATE

CANONGATE BOOKS PS

Voted UK Publisher of the Year in 2009, Canongate is one of Britain's leading independent houses, publishing literary fiction and non-fiction from around the world.

Recent fiction successes include Nick Cave's *The Death of Bunny Munro* (including a tailor-made iPhone app version), Rebecca Miller's *The Private Lives of Pippa Lee* (a Richard & Judy Summer Read 2008), Scarlett Thomas's *The End of Mr. Y*, Steven Hall's *The Raw Shark Texts* and Andrew Davidson's internationally-acclaimed debut *The Gargoyle*.

Our non-fiction triumphs include *The Audacity of Hope* and *Dreams From My Father* by Barack Obama (also available as Enhanced Edition iPhone apps), Neil Strauss's *The Game* and *The Rules of the Game*, *Homicide* – the true crime classic from *The Wire* creator David Simon – and *The Mighty Book of Boosh*, the official tie-in to the award-winning television series.

Canongate is the publisher of *Life of Pi*, the bestselling Booker-winner to date. The reissue campaign was a winner of the Book Marketing Society's Best Marketing Campaigns award May-August 2009, and the illustrated version won a prestigious British Book Design and Production Award in 2008. Other prize-winning authors include Kate Grenville and MJ Hyland (both Booker-shortlisted), James Meek, Michel Faber, Louise Welsh and Anne Donovan.

Established: 1994 (under present name)
Publications (yearly average): 70
Types of books published: Fiction; biography; general non-fiction
Submission details: We accept unsolicited manuscripts in the form of a synopsis, sample chapters and a self-addressed, stamped envelope. We do not accept submissions via email.

CONTACTS
People: Jamie Byng (Managing Director); Anya Serota (Publishing Director); Polly Collingridge (Rights Director); Caroline Gorham (Production Director); Jenny Todd (Sales and Marketing Director); Nick Davies (Editorial Director, Non-fiction); Kathleen Anderson (Finance Director); Norah Perkins (Managing Editor); Dan Franklin (Digital Editor)
Address: 14 High Street, Edinburgh EH1 1TE
Tel: 0131 557 5111
Fax: 0131 557 5211
Email: info@canongate.co.uk
Website: www.meetatthegate.com
Distributor: The Book Service Ltd (TBS), Frating Green, Colchester, Essex, CO7 7DW; keyaccounts@tbs-ltd.co.uk; Tel: 01206 256 060; Fax: 01206 255 914

Chapman
Scotland's Quality Literary Magazine

CHAPMAN PUBLISHING LTD (CHAPMAN MAGAZINE) PS

Chapman is Scotland's leading literary magazine, controversial, intelligent and full of surprises. Founded in 1970, it is a dynamic force in Scottish culture, publishing new poetry, fiction, criticism and reviews. *Chapman* also covers theatre, politics, language and the arts in a probing, enlightened manner.

The latest in Scottish writing appears in *Chapman*'s pages – new work by well-known writers and also many lesser known, Scottish mainly, but increasingly international, some of whom then make considerable impact in the literary scene. But not content with passive publishing, the magazine pursues a proactive cultural agenda, progressing the cultural debate in Scotland.

The *Chapman* New Writing Series further promotes talented writers from the magazine. Notably successful is its Wild Women Series, featuring Magi Gibson's *Wild Women of a Certain Age*, Janet Paisley's *Alien Crop* and *Ye Cannae Win*, all of which are now in reprint. This venture has helped many writers progress to a new stage in their careers. The most recent publication is *Winter Barley* by Caithness poet George Gunn.

Established: Magazine – 1970; book publishing – 1986
Publications: 1–2 per annum
Types of books published: Literary, arts and culture magazine; books – mainly poetry, occasionally shorter fiction and drama
Submission Details: Submissions to *Chapman* magazine always welcome – see website for guidelines. Any writer hoping for book publication should begin by first submitting work to the magazine.

CONTACTS
People: Joy Hendry (Editor)
Address: 4 Broughton Place, Edinburgh EH1 3RX
Tel: 0131 557 2207
Email: chapman-pub@blueyonder.co.uk
Website: www.chapman-pub.co.uk

COMHAIRLE NAN LEABHRAICHEAN/THE GAELIC BOOKS COUNCIL PS

The Council was set up to assist and stimulate Gaelic publishing. Originally part of Glasgow University, it became a separate charitable company in 1996, and has a board of nine (a Scottish Arts Council assessor also attends meetings) and a paid staff of four. The SAC has been its main funding body since 1983, and in recent years Bòrd na Gàidhlig has become an essential funder also.

The Council provides publication grants (paid to the publisher) for individual Gaelic books submitted before publication and operates a scheme of commission grants for books as yet unwritten. Its bookshop stocks all Gaelic and Gaelic-related titles in print and there is a mail order service, as well as special sales at events such as Mods, conferences and weekend courses. Titles stocked are detailed in the paper catalogue, Leabhraichean Gàidhlig, and the website. A free editorial and advisory service is also available.

Company established: 1968
Types of books published: Catalogues and book news magazines; poetry posters

CONTACTS
People: Ian MacDonald (Director)
Address: 22 Mansfield Street, Glasgow G11 5QP
Tel: 0141 337 6211
Email: brath@gaelicbooks.net
Fax: 0141 341 0515
Websites: www.gaelicbooks.org and www.ur-sgeul.com
Distributor: Comhairle nan Leabhraichean/The Gaelic Books Council

CONTINUING EDUCATION GATEWAY PS

Gateway is a distinctive, cross-media organisation. We provide a unique range of services, including websites and publications to support career and education services throughout Scotland.

Gateway's researchers and editors collate information about learning opportunities and careers throughout Scotland to produce a comprehensive range of annually updated reference books. These are used extensively by professionals (careers advisers, subject teachers and pastoral care staff) in schools, colleges, Careers Scotland Centres and other organisations. They are available also to individual pupils and their parents or carers in libraries and community settings.

Established: 1989
Publications (yearly average): 4
Types of books published: Our current titles include: *Careers in Scotland*: an essential guide to full time courses at Scottish colleges and universities. This comprehensive directory has detailed information on courses from Access to taught postgraduate level, including entry requirements.

Its two companion volumes focus on a specific range of courses: *Further Education in Scotland* (Access to HNC) and *Higher Education in Scotland* (HND and above). The three directories also contain general information on important topics such as finance for study.

We also produce *Job Seeking Skills*: the young job hunter's guide to finding and getting into a job. This is a practical workbook used extensively by school leavers and their advisers as a source of valuable support on issues such as sourcing vacancies, telephone techniques, job search letters, application forms, interview techniques, CVs and more.

CONTACTS
People: Linda Wilkie
Address: 199 Nithsdale Road, Glasgow G41 5EX
Tel: 0141 422 1070
Fax: 0141 422 2919
Email: ceg@ceg.org.uk
Website: www.ceg.org.uk
Distributor: Continuing Education Gateway

Dionysia Press

DIONYSIA PRESS LTD PS

Dionysia Press has published award-winning poets, such as Susanna Roxman, who received the Lund's Award in Sweden for her collection *Broken Angels*, and award-winning translations, notably Thom Nairn's and D Zervanou's translation *The Complete Poems of George Vafopoulos*. This collection received the first award for best translation for the year 1999, by the Hellenic Association for Translation.

Dionysia Press has published numerous outstanding writers including Thom Nairn, Edwin Morgan, Tom Bryan, R Leach, Stuart Campbell, Alexis Stamatis, Byron Leodaris, Manolis Pratikakis, Andreas Mitsou, D Zervanou, Nikos Davvetas, Kyriakos Charalabidis, many of whom have received major awards and commendations.

Company established: 1989
Publications to date: 51
Types of books published: Poetry, translations, novels, short stories

CONTACTS
People: Denise Smith (Director)
Address: 7 Duddingston House Courtyard, 127 Milton Road West, Edinburgh EH15 1JG
Fax: 0131 656 9565
Website: dionysiapress.wordpress.com
Distributor: Dionysia Press Ltd

DUDU NSOMBA PUBLICATIONS PS

Dudu Nsomba Publications specialise in writing on and about Malawi, in particular, and Africa, in general. Over the last 16 years it has built up a reputation as an innovative, independent and boundary-pushing publisher. Our emphasis is on content rather than countenance; book publishing without frills or make up.

We cover politics, literature, economics, music, novels, poetry, short stories and religion. The sister company, Pamtondo, publishes music.

Established: 1993
Publications to date: 17

CONTACTS
People: John Lwanda (Managing Director)
Address: 5c Greystone Avenue, Rutherglen, Glasgow G73 3SN
Tel: 0141 647 5195
Fax: 0141 647 5195
Mobile: 07860 629 480
Email: lwanda2000@yahoo.co.uk and johnlwanda@msn.com
Website: www.pamtondo.com
Distributor: Various

DUNDEE CITY COUNCIL LEISURE & COMMUNITIES DEPARTMENT AND EDUCATION DEPARTMENT PS

In partnership these departments promote literacy and reading in exciting and innovative ways. In 2006 we published *Time Tram Dundee* to address the lack of local history information for young people which was accessible and fun.

In 2004 we established the Dundee Picture Book Award which carries a substantial cash prize for the creators of the winning title. Each year approximately 800 children are involved in voting for their favourite picture book from a shortlist of four titles.

2008 saw a unique competition for all our S1 and S2 pupils who were challenged to write the blurb for a book they would like to see in print. The prize was that Catherine MacPhail would write the book of the winning blurb and Barrington Stoke would publish it. 1,500 entries were received and the competition attracted interest from across the country. The project was Highly Commended in the Standard Life Creative Sparks Competition.

In 2009 *Hide and Seek*, the book from the blurb competition was published by Barrington Stoke.

Also in 2009, a project we had piloted was rolled out to 10 schools in Dundee. This aims to get girls into science and boys into books. It involves using the Barrington Stoke title *Crazy Creatures* by Gill Arbuthnott and is a partnership between Dundee City Council, Sensation Science Centre and the University of Dundee. The project is being used as a case study by HMIe and has been short-listed for the Association of Scottish Visitor Attractions *Big Idea* award.

CONTACTS
People: Stuart Syme (tel: 01382 431 546); School Library Service, Central Library, The Wellgate, Dundee, DD1 1DB; Email: stuart.syme@dundeecity.gov.uk
and
Moira Foster (tel: 01382 434 888); Educational Development Service, Lawton Road, Dundee, DD3 6SY; Email: moira.foster@dundeecity.gov.uk
Website: www.dundeecity.gov.uk/library
Distributor: BookSource, 50 Cambuslang Road, Glasgow, G32 8NB;
Tel: 0845 3700 063; Email: info@booksource.net

DUNEDIN ACADEMIC PRESS LTD PS

Established in 2000, Dunedin Academic Press Ltd (Dunedin) is an independent academic and professional publishing house. Dunedin has as its main object the publication of first class works of scholarship and utility, usually for audiences at undergraduate level and upward.

Dunedin's list will always reflect its Scottish location. However, the list contains authors and subjects from the international academic world and Dunedin's horizons are far broader than our immediate Scottish environment. One of our strengths is that we provide our authors the individual support that comes from dealing with a small independent publisher committed to growth.

Dunedin welcomes approaches from new academic authors particularly in the fields of earth science, education practice and policy and the health and social sciences. Our proposal guidelines can be found on our website.

Established: 2000
Publications (yearly average): 18
Types of books published: Earth science, social science, philosophy, education, health and social care, history, Gaelic studies, and vocal studies
Submission details: See proposal guidelines on our website

CONTACTS
People: Anthony Kinahan (Director), Norman Steven (Finance Director)
Address: Hudson House, 8 Albany Street, Edinburgh EH1 3QB
Tel: 0131 473 2397
Fax: 01250 870 920
Email: mail@dunedinacademicpress.co.uk
Website: www.dunedinacademicpress.co.uk
Distributor: Turpin Distribution, Pegasus Drive, Stratton Business Park, Biggleswade, SG18 8TQ; Tel: 01767 604 951; Fax: 01767 601 640

East Lothian
Library Services
read • click • listen • discover

EAST LOTHIAN LIBRARY SERVICE PS

East Lothian Library Service provides a public library service. Running a busy enquiry and research service on local history and genealogy, we are well placed to identify topics of interest within the area. We publish occasional adult non-fiction titles for those interested in the local history of the area, its towns and villages. East Lothian Local History Centre also provides resources for authors working on local research. These include a large photograph collection, books and maps.

The Service publishes *East Lothian 1945–2000* in 7 volumes. Volume 1 gives an overview of the county, while volumes 2–6 each cover an area of parishes. They blend historical detail, with descriptions written by local people, to provide an update to the statistical accounts. The final volume dealing with childhood in East Lothian will be launched in November 2009. Other publications can be found on our website.

CONTACTS
People: Sheila Millar (Senior Librarian: Local History and Promotions)
Address: Library Headquarters, Dunbar Road, Haddington EH41 3PJ
Tel: 01620 828 200
Fax: 01620 828 201
Email: smillar@eastlothian.gov.uk
Website: www.eastlothian.gov.uk
Website for publications: http://localpublications.notlong.com
Distributor: East Lothian Council Library Service

CULTURE AND LEISURE

EDINBURGH CITY LIBRARIES/SERVICES FOR COMMUNITIES DEPARTMENT, CITY OF EDINBURGH COUNCIL PS

Edinburgh City Libraries provides a public library service, offering books, newspapers, periodicals and electronic resources for study and loan. We support the independent learner, as well as the recreational user, in 26 locations across the city, plus services to prisons, hospitals and other institutions.

We publish infrequently, but we provide web access to digital copies of many rare and valuable images, photographs and prints of contemporary and historic Edinburgh, which can also be bought as hard copies. This is a valuable resource for researchers, authors and publishers.

We have won several awards for our innovative work with young people, including Libraries Change Lives, Great Scot Community Champion Award, Standing up to Anti-social Behaviour, APSE Award for Best Service team, Outstanding Public services Team of the Year and others.

Established: 1890
Publications (yearly average): 1
Types of books published: Books; booklets; prints; greeting cards

CONTACTS
Address: Level C:4, Waverley Court, 4 East Market Street, Edinburgh EH8 8BG
Tel: 0131 200 2000
Email: eclas@edinburgh.gov.uk
Website: www.edinburgh.gov.uk/libraries
Distributor: Edinburgh City Libraries

EDINBURGH UNIVERSITY PRESS [PS]

Edinburgh University Press is the premier scholarly publisher in Scotland of academic books and journals and one of the leading university presses in the UK.

Founded over fifty years ago, Edinburgh University Press became a wholly owned subsidiary of the University of Edinburgh in 1992. Books and journals published by the Press carry the imprimatur of one of Britain's oldest and most distinguished centres of learning and enjoy the highest academic standards through the scholarly appraisal of the Press Committee. Since August 2004 the Press has had charitable status, charity number SC 035813.

We are committed to furthering knowledge and making innovative and rigorous scholarship available to the widest possible readership through our range of research publications. These include scholarly monographs and reference works as well as materials which are available online. The Press also plays a prominent educational role by providing stimulating, well-designed textbooks for students and lecturers.

The Press seeks excellence in its chosen subjects combining high quality scholarship and commerciality to produce academic works of lasting value.

Established: 1946
Publications (yearly average): 110
Types of books published: Our main subject areas across our books and journals programmes are: African studies, American studies, classics, critical editions, film and media studies, historical studies, Islamic studies, language and linguistics, law, literary studies, philosophy, politics, reference, religion, science and medical, Scottish studies
Submission details: see www.euppublishing.com/page/infoZone/authors/BookProposal

CONTACTS
Address: 22 George Square, Edinburgh EH8 9LF
Tel: 0131 650 4218
Fax: 0131 650 3286
Email (editorial): editorial@eup.ed.ac.uk
Email (marketing): marketing@eup.ed.ac.uk
Email (journals): journals@eup.ed.ac.uk
Website: www.euppublishing.com
Distributor: Marston Book Services Ltd, 160 Milton Park, Abingdon, Oxon OX14 4SD; Tel: 01235 465 500; Fax: 01235 465 509

FIDRA BOOKS LTD PS

We are an independent publishing company specialising in rescuing neglected children's fiction and making it available to a new generation of readers. Our books range from 1940s adventure stories to iconic 1960s fantasy novels and from pony books by Carnegie medal winning authors to rare boarding school stories from the 1990s. We value high production quality, which makes our titles popular with collectors; however, they are popular with nostalgia buyers, school libraries, and children themselves.

We are booksellers as well as publishers: we own Edinburgh's only specialist children's bookshop, in which we combine a wall of our titles with what we consider to be the best in contemporary children's fiction and non-fiction titles. We have also just opened The Edinburgh Bookshop for grown-ups, where we pride ourselves in stocking an eclectic range of books we love.

Established: 2005
Submission details: We do not take submissions for new work, because we specialise in republishing classics.

CONTACTS
People: Vanessa Robertson (Managing Director); Dr Malcolm Robertson (Director)
Address: The Children's Bookshop, 219 Bruntsfield Place, Edinburgh EH10 4DH
Tel: 0131 447 1917
Email: info@fidrabooks.co.uk
Website: www.fidrabooks.co.uk
Distributor: Fidra Books and Gardners Books Ltd, 1 Whittle Drive, Eastbourne, East Sussex, BN23 6QH; Tel: 01323 521 777

FLEDGLING PRESS PS

Fledgling Press was founded to make talented new authors available to readers quickly and effectively in a variety of formats – downloadable e-books and short-run printed books in the main – and to give readers, authors, and site visitors an exciting and fulfilling experience. Talent is subjectively defined as the ability to lure me along with high quality writing into an extension of my experience that enriches and deepens my life, and has the potential to do this for many others. In practice, historical and crime fiction have dominated my list, with some autobiography, poetry, short stories, and a cookbook or three.

Company established: 2000; imprint established 1993
Publications (yearly average): 2–4
Submission guidelines: Email submission of a synopsis and two sample chapters to zander@fledglingpress.co.uk is preferred. Paper proposals should be similar and need a reply-paid envelope if you want them to be returned.

CONTACTS
People: Zander Wedderburn
Address: 7 Lennox Street (GF), Edinburgh EH4 1QB
Tel: 0131 343 2367
Email: zander@fledglingpress.co.uk
Website: www.fledglingpress.co.uk and www.canyouwrite.com
Distributor: zander@fledglingpress.co.uk

FLORIS BOOKS ⓅⓈ

At Floris Books we see the world a little differently. Our adult non-fiction books cover all aspects of holistic and alternative living, including holistic health, organics and the environment, holistic education, mind body spirit, child health and development, self-help, religion and spirituality, and community living.

We're also the largest children's book publisher in Scotland, producing international picture books, story books and children's fiction. Our Kelpies range of Scottish novels includes works by both classic children's novelists and contemporary authors. The annual Kelpies Prize was set up to encourage and reward new Scottish writing for children. Winners include *Hox* by Annemarie Allan and *Magnus Fin and the Ocean Quest* by Janis Mackay. Kelpies Prize runner-up *First Aid for Fairies and Other Fabled Beasts* by Lari Don won a Royal Mail Scottish Children's Book Award 2009.

New for 2010: Floris Books will be launching the Picture Kelpies, a range of children's picture books with strong Scottish themes and settings, created by new and established authors and illustrators.

Established: 1977
Types of books published: Celtic studies; education; science; alternative living; self-help; mind, body and spirit; children's novels; children's picture books; religion; craft and activity
Submission details: Send a synopsis and the first three chapters. We only accept children's book submissions with strong Scottish settings or themes. Please see our website for guidelines on Kelpies Prize submissions.

CONTACTS
People: Christian Maclean (Manager); Christopher Moore (Commissioning Editor); Sally Martin (Senior Commissioning Editor); Catherine McKinney (Production Manager); Angela Smith (Publishing Assistant); Katy Lockwood-Holmes (Sales and Marketing Manager/Deputy Publisher); Chani McBain (Sales and Marketing Executive)
Address: 15 Harrison Gardens, Edinburgh EH11 1SH
Tel: 0131 337 2372
Fax: 0131 347 9919
Email: floris@florisbooks.co.uk
Website: www.florisbooks.co.uk
Distributor: BookSource, 50 Cambuslang Road, Cambuslang, Glasgow G32 8NB; Tel: 0845 370 0067; Fax: 0845 370 0068. Also distributor for Lindisfarne Press.

Forestry Commission

FORESTRY COMMISSION ⓅⓈ

The Forestry Commission is the government department responsible for protecting and expanding Britain's forests and woodlands. It is a world leader in the development of sustainable forestry and it publishes a wide range of information and guidance in support of the UK Forestry Standard and the Science and Innovation Strategy for British Forestry. The Forestry Commission is the largest single land manager in Britain and the guardian of some of its most beautiful forest and woodland habitats. As well as producing wood, it is the biggest single provider of outdoor recreation, and it works closely with a wide range of partners to further its aims of increasing the value of forests and woodlands to society and the environment.

Established: 1919
Types of books published: Environment/science and forestry/land management

CONTACTS
People: Elaine Dick (Publications Manager)
Tel: 0131 334 0303
Email: elaine.dick@forestry.gsi.gov.uk
Website: www.forestry.gov.uk/publications
Distributor: Forestry Commission Publications, PO Box 25, Wetherby, West Yorkshire LS23 7EW; Tel: 0844 991 6500 ; Fax: 0844 991 9501; Email: forestry@mrm.co.uk

WAVERLEY
BOOKS

GEDDES AND GROSSET; WAVERLEY BOOKS PS

An established, innovative publisher of popular reference, children's and trade books (trade under Waverley). Reference books are produced primarily for the mass-market and export. The Waverley list includes books for the Scottish trade market such as the best-selling *Maw Broon's Cookbooks* and related titles. Waverley also published the graphic novels *Kidnapped* and *Jekyll and Hyde* by Cam Kennedy and Alan Grant. *Lost Railways of Scotland, Mein Rant, Maw Broon's Remedies, The Glasgow Cookery Book,* and *The Broons' Gairdenin' Wisdoms* are lead titles for 2009.

Established: 1988
Publications (yearly average): 20 titles (backlist 500+ titles)
Types of books published: Reference books; children's books; regional interest books and books as premiums and incentives
Submission details: Non-fiction/general reference by letter and synopsis with sample chapter to Liz Small (no unsolicited fiction submissions can be accepted)

CONTACTS
People: Ron Grosset, Mike Miller, Liz Small
Address: 144 Port Dundas Road, Glasgow G4 0HZ
Tel: 0141 567 2830
Fax: 0141 567 2831 **Email:** info@gandg.sol.co.uk; info@waverley-books.co.uk
Website: www.geddesandgrosset.co.uk; www.waverley-books.co.uk
Distributor of Geddes and Grosset: Peter Haddock Ltd, Pinfold Lane, Bridlington, Yorkshire YO16 6BT; Tel: 01262 678 121; Fax: 01262 400 043
Distributor of Waverley Books: BookSource, 50 Cambuslang Road, Cambuslang, Glasgow G32 8NB; Tel: 0845 370 0067; Fax: 0845 370 0068

GLASGOW CITY LIBRARIES PUBLICATIONS PS

Glasgow City Libraries Publications produce publications of Glasgow interest or related to material held in the Mitchell Library.

Company established: 1980
Titles in print: Over 30 with one as co-publisher and more than 20 library bibliographies

CONTACTS
Address: The Mitchell Library, North Street, Glasgow G3 7DN
Tel: 0141 287 2809
Fax: 0141 287 2815
Email: Maureen.wilbraham@csglasgow.org
Distributor: The Mitchell Library

Glasgow|museums

GLASGOW MUSEUMS PUBLISHING PS

We have a long history of publishing – Kelvingrove Art Gallery and Museum opened in 1901, and people have been writing about and publishing on the city's collections ever since. The focus of Glasgow Museums Publishing programme is naturally the one million plus objects held in these collections, but we also publish educational materials and on local history and archaeology. Recent bestsellers include *Glasgow 1955: Through the lens*, a collection of photographs taken by camera clubs around the city in 1955; and *Archaeology Around Glasgow: 50 remarkable sites to visit* (in conjunction with Glasgow Archaeological Society). We welcome proposals for co-publishing projects.

Established: 1901
Publications (yearly average): 5
Types of books published: Art, guidebooks to collections, local history and archaeology, educational materials
Submission details: Please contact us before sending any material

CONTACTS
People: Susan Pacitti, Managing Editor (sales, editorial, publicity)
Address: Glasgow Museums Publishing, Culture and Sport Glasgow, Glasgow Museums Resource Centre, 200 Woodhead Road, Glasgow G53 7NN
Tel: 0141 276 9452
Fax: 0141 276 9305
Email: susan.pacitti@csglasgow.org
Website: www.glasgowmuseums.com
Distributor: BookSource (from late 2009)

THE GLENEIL PRESS PS

We publish our own Clan history, *The Clan Gleneil*. Creative and evocative in the spirit of Sir Walter Scott, it encapsulates the essence of Scotland and the best aspects of the Clan system. Available direct from the publisher in hardcover (£10 including p&p within the UK), it entitles the buyer to wear the attractive Clan tartan obtainable from Lochcarron of Scotland in Selkirk. As our history explains, all Clan tartans were banned after 1745 and most patterns destroyed. Interest in Clan tartans only revived slowly after George IV's historic visit to Scotland in 1822 (see illustration pp 43–44 *The Clan Gleneil*) and tartans are still being created and registered.

We mainly publish books of Scottish interest, such as *The Scottish Highlanders & Their Regiments*, but also many others with wide appeal, for example *The Making of The English Gentleman Trilogy* published in October 2009. In preparation is a 'Travels-over-Time' series, covering mainly Scotland.

Established:1995
Publications:12. The annual average varies. Mainly non-fiction; military history, travel, biography, food and drink
Submission details: No unsolicited manuscripts accepted.

CONTACTS
Address: The Gleneil Press, Whittingehame Mains, East Lothian, EH41 4QA
Tel: 01620 860 292
Email: gleneilpress@tiscali.co.uk
Website: www.gleneil.com
Distributor: The Gleneil Press

GOBLINSHEAD

GOBLINSHEAD PS

Goblinshead publishes popular and tourist books on Scottish history, castles, biographies, architecture, prehistory and Scottish fiction.

Established: 1994
Submission details: Scottish interest, history, including fiction. No submissions accepted until discussed with staff. Please contact by email (goblinshead@sol. co.uk) or by phone.

CONTACTS
People: Martin Coventry
Address: 130b Inveresk Road, Musselburgh EH21 7AY
Tel: 0131 665 2894
Fax: 0131 653 6566
Email: goblinshead@sol.co.uk
Distributor: Goblinshead

GRACE NOTE PUBLICATIONS [PS]

Grace Note Publications CIC (Community Interest Company) is committed to publishing books and audio resources in Gaelic and Scots, to help support Scotland's indigenous languages and culture.
• The resources aim to create good models of language and speech to help to retain the high standards of language set by previous generations and to maintain these standards of speech in everyday conversation.
• To give opportunities to writers and musicians rooted in Scotland's indigenous languages to promote their high standard work in everyday speech, education, the arts and media.

Established: 2007
Types of books and recordings published: Scottish folklore; traditional culture; children's books; short stories. All books and audio productions should have at least 50% in Scottish Gaelic or Scots, or a combination of both languages.
Submission details: Send GNP a short summary of the project to the address below

CONTACTS
People: Gonzalo Mazzei (Manager); Luise Valentiner/Trigger Press (Artistic Director); Margaret Bennett (Independent Advisor)
Address: Grange of Locherlour, Ochtertyre, by Crieff, Perthshire PH7 4JS.
Tel: 01764 655 979
Email: books@gracenotereading.co.uk
Distributor: Highlander Music, Unit 7D, Muir Of Ord Industrial Estate, Rossshire IV6 7UA, Tel: 01463 871 422; Fax: 01463 871 433. Also distributed by The Gaelic Books Council, 22 Mansfield Street, Glasgow G11 5QP; Tel: 0141 337 6211.

HACHETTE SCOTLAND

Hachette Scotland is an imprint of Hachette UK which publishes a small list of Scottish-originated fiction and non-fiction.

We publish 10–12 high-quality commercial titles a year, focusing on new talent and established names. The list specialises in sport, cookery/lifestyle, autobiography/memoir, humour, history, and in genre, reading group and literary fiction. Titles published so far include:

- *Daisychain* – the debut thriller from Glasgow-based lawyer GJ Moffat
- *A Shirt Box Full Of Songs* – The autobiography of the popular singer and actress Barbara Dickson
- *The Official Rangers Hall of Fame* – a celebration of the Rangers players who have been inducted into The Hall of Fame
- *Death of a Ladies' Man – The third novel from acclaimed novelist Alan Bissett*
- *Whose Turn for the Stairs?* – the fiction debut of Robert Douglas, the author of the best-selling *Night Song of the Last Tram*
- *Taste Ye Back* – the latest book from Sue Lawrence in which she talks to a number of prominent Scots about their childhood food memories.

CONTACTS

People: Bob McDevitt, Publisher (tel: 0141 552 8082; mobile 07876 508 716)
Address: 2a Christie Street, Paisley PA1 1NB
Email: bob.mcdevitt@hachettescotland.co.uk
Types of books published: Scottish interest books: both fiction (crime, literary, other genre) and non-fiction (sport, biography, travel, history, TV tie-ins, humour, cookery) but not children's, religious, poetry or educational titles
Distributor: Bookpoint, 130 Milton Park, Abingdon, OX14 4SB; Tel: 01235 400 400

Hallewell
Publications

HALLEWELL PUBLICATIONS `PS`

Hallewell Publications is a small publishing house which concentrates largely on a single project: a series of walking guides covering Scotland and the north of England. We currently have 43 titles in print (for a full list, please visit www.pocketwalks.com). Most of the guides are currently written by ourselves and we initiate all publications – sorry, no submissions.

Established: 1995
Publications (yearly average): 3–4
Types of books published: Guide books, walking
Submission details: No unsolicited manuscripts

CONTACTS
People: Richard Hallewell, Rebecca Hallewell
Address: The Milton, Foss, Pitlochry, Perthshire PH16 5NQ
Tel/Fax: 01882 634 254
Email: hallewell-pubs@btconnect.com
Website: www.pocketwalks.com
Distributor: BookSource, 50 Cambuslang Road, Cambuslang, Glasgow G32 8NB; Tel: 0845 370 0067; Fax: 0845 370 0068

▦ HarperCollins*Publishers*

HARPERCOLLINS PUBLISHERS PS

HarperCollins UK publishes a wide range of books, from cutting-edge contemporary fiction, to block-busting thrillers, from fantasy literature and children's stories to enduring classics. It also publishes a great selection of non-fiction titles, including history, celebrity memoirs, biographies, popular science, dictionaries, maps, reference titles and education books, and its digital business is thriving. With nearly 200 years of history, HarperCollins publishes some of the world's foremost authors, from Nobel Prize winners to worldwide bestsellers. In addition it publishes the works of Agatha Christie, JRR Tolkien and CS Lewis. It was the first major UK trade publisher to go carbon neutral in December 2007.

Established: 1819
Submission details: All fiction and trade non-fiction must be submitted through an agent, or unsolicited manuscripts may be submitted through the online writing community at www.authonomy.com
Types of books published: popular and literary fiction; non-fiction; biography; history; dictionaries and reference; children's; bibles; educational; sport; travel; home and leisure; and cartographic

CONTACTS
People: Victoria Barnsley (CEO and Publisher), Belinda Budge (Publisher)
Bishopbriggs address: Westerhill Road, Bishopbriggs, Glasgow G64 2QT
Tel: 0141 772 3200
Fax: 0141 306 3119
London address: 77–85 Fulham Palace Road, London W6 8JB
Tel: 020 8741 7070
Fax: 020 8307 4440
E-mail: firstname.secondname@ harpercollins.co.uk
Website: www.harpercollins.co.uk
Distributor: HarperCollins Publishers (Trade), Customer Services Department, Campsie View, Westerhill Road, Bishopbriggs, Glasgow, G64 2QT;
Tel: 0870 787 1722; Fax: 0870 787 993

HODDER
GIBSON
Educational Publishers
for Scotland

HODDER GIBSON PS

Hodder Gibson publishes the widest and largest range of textbooks and revision guides aimed specifically at the Scottish secondary curriculum, as well as a number of titles for Scottish primary schools and continuing professional development for Scottish teachers. We also publish a growing number of electronic support materials based on our *Dynamic Learning* engine for interactive learning.

We won the Times Educational Supplement Scotland/Saltire Society Award for Educational Book of the Year on no fewer than eight occasions in the competition's twelve-year history, and were commended or highly commended in three of the other four years.

As well as long-standing traditional texts (such as *The New First Aid in English*, a book first published in 1938), we offer attractive and motivating titles that aim to enhance learning for today's students. The majority of our school textbooks are published in full colour, and our award-winning *How to Pass* range, endorsed by the Scottish Qualifications Authority, provides up-to-date revision materials across all three examination levels of Standard Grade, Intermediate and Higher.

Established: 2002 (part of Hodder Education), Hodder Education established 1906, Robert Gibson established 1874
Publications (yearly average): 30
Types of books published: Educational textbooks and revision guides for the Scottish curriculum
Submission details: Contact John Mitchell or Katherine Bennett in the first instance

CONTACTS
People: John Mitchell (Managing Director); Katherine Bennett (Commissioning Editor); Elizabeth Hayes (Project Editor); Jim Donnelly (Scottish Sales Manager); Jim Chalmers (Trade Sales)
Address: 2a Christie Street, Paisley PA1 1NB
Tel: 0141 848 1609
Fax: 0141 889 6315
Email: hoddergibson@hodder.co.uk
Website: www.hoddergibson.co.uk
Distributor: Bookpoint, 130 Milton Park, Abingdon OX14 4SB; Tel: 01235 400 400

Leckie×Leckie

Scotland's leading educational publishers

LECKIE & LECKIE PS

Founded in 1989, Leckie & Leckie is Scotland's leading educational publisher, with a list of over 200 revision guides specifically for Scottish secondary education students. Published principally in a full colour A4 format, our tried and tested books have been the first choice for hundreds of thousands of successful Scottish students.

We specialise in revision guides and course notes for Scotland's national qualifications, focusing on exactly what students need to know to pass their exams. In 2009 Leckie & Leckie introduced a new series to the educational market: Practice Papers for SQA Exams - brand new exam-style questions with fully-worked answer sections, marking schemes, topic indexes and revision tips and advice, showing students exactly what examiners are looking for and how to aim for the best grade.

Also in 2009, Leckie & Leckie introduced the first series dedicated to implementing A Curriculum for Excellence called ACTIVE Learning. This is a range of Course Notes and Workbooks for S1 to S3, available for a range of subject areas.

Broadly available in bookshops and bought by students and parents, the Leckie & Leckie range of books is also widely adopted by teachers for school use throughout Scotland.

Established: 1989
Publications (yearly average): 20
Types of books published: Scottish teaching, learning and revision
Submission details: We accept unsolicited manuscripts

CONTACTS
People: Martin Redfern (Publishing Director) and Sarah Falconer (Sales and Marketing Manager)
Address: 4 Queen Street, Edinburgh EH2 1JE
Tel: 0131 220 6831
Fax: 0131 225 9987
Email: enquiries@leckieandleckie.co.uk
Website: www.leckieandleckie.co.uk
Distributor: Leckie & Leckie, HarperCollins, Customer Services Department, Westerhill Road, Bishopbriggs, Glasgow, G64 2QT; Tel: 0870 460 7662; Fax: 0870 787 1720

LUATH PRESS LTD PS

Luath Press takes its name from Robert Burns, whose little collie Luath (Gael., swift or nimble) tripped up Jean Armour at a wedding and gave him the chance to speak to the woman who was to be his wife and the abiding love of his life. Burns called one of 'The Twa Dogs' Luath after Cuchullin's hunting dog in Ossian's Fingal. Luath Press was established in 1981 in the heart of Burns country, and is now based a few steps up the road from Burns' first lodgings on Edinburgh's Royal Mile.

Luath Press is an independent publishing house which offers distinctive writing with a hint of unexpected pleasures. Prizewinning and shortlisted books include *Bad Catholics* (Specsavers Crime Writers Association New Blood Dagger – shortlisted) and *The Bower Bird* by Ann Kelley (Costa Children's Book Award – winner; UK Literacy Association Book Award – winner).

Established: 1981
Publications (yearly average): 50
Types of books published: Committed to publishing well-written books worth reading. Subjects covered include: fiction; history; guide books; walking; poetry; art; humour; biography; natural history; current issues and much more.
Submission details: Anything from a tentative phone call to a complete manuscript (including introduction, author profile, synopsis etc) welcome – we are delighted to have the opportunity to discuss/ explore potential projects with any individual or organisation, preferably (but not exclusively) based in Scotland.

CONTACTS
People: Gavin MacDougall (Director)
Address: 543/2 Castlehill, The Royal Mile, Edinburgh EH1 2ND
Tel: 0131 225 4326
Fax: 0131 225 4324
Email: gavin.macdougall@luath.co.uk
Website: www.luath.co.uk
Distributor: [UK] HarperCollins Third Party Distribution, Westerhill Road, Bishopbriggs, Glasgow G64 2QT; Tel: 0870 787 1722; Fax: 0870 787 1723
[USA & Canada] Ingram Publisher Services, 1 Ingram Blvd, La Vergne, TN 37086, USA, Tel. 001 866 400 5351, Fax 001 800 838 1149

MAINSTREAM PUBLISHING 🅿🅢

Mainstream Publishing was established in 1978 and has gone on to become one of Scotland's leading publishers of non-fiction. In 2005, Mainstream entered an exciting new partnership with Random House and since then has had four Sunday Times bestsellers with *Ashes Fever*, *Don't Ever Tell*, *Someone to Watch Over Me* and *Ma, He Sold Me for a Few Cigarettes*. Mainstream is based in Edinburgh's New Town and continues to pride itself on publishing good books about Scotland. *Nothing But a Dame* by Elaine C Smith and *Goalie* by Andy Goram are both high profile Scottish books which have been published recently and *Scotland's Music* is a lavish tome that we are delighted to have brought back into print.

Company established: 1978
Titles in print: 700+
Types of books published: General non-fiction; biography; autobiography; art; photography; health; sport; guidebooks; travel; true crime
Submission details: Synopsis and sample chapters in the first instance. Supply a SAE or return postage if manuscript is to be returned.

CONTACTS
People: Bill Campbell (Joint Managing Director); Peter MacKenzie (Joint Managing Director); Fiona Brownlee (Marketing and Rights Director); Neil Graham (Production Manager); Ailsa Bathgate (Editorial Director)
Address: 7 Albany Street, Edinburgh EH1 3UG
Tel: 0131 557 2959
Email: enquiries@mainstreampublishing.com
Fax: 0131 556 8720
Distributor: TBS, Frating Distribution Centre, Colchester Road, Frating Green, Colchester, Essex CO7 7DW; Tel: 01206 256000; Fax: 01206 255715

MOONLIGHT PUBLISHING LTD ᴘꜱ

Moonlight Publishing was founded in 1980 to create a new kind of information book for young children. From the start our aim was to explain how things work and how different facts are related to one another, why the world is as it is and why people and things interact in everyday life as they do.

Discovery has always been the theme behind our publishing and most of our series are named accordingly. Our most successful series, First Discovery, has sold over 40 million copies in 30 languages around the world, which proves that these books have a universal appeal.

Although we are a small independent company run by only two people, John and Penny Clement, we operate all over the world through publishing partnerships.

The majority of our readers are repeat buyers; many collect our series. Many customers buy direct from us because they can't find the full range of our books in bookshops.

Established: 1980
Types of books published: Children's illustrated non-fiction
Submission details: We do not accept unsolicited manuscripts

CONTACTS
People: John Clement (Managing Director)
Address: The King's Manor, East Hendred, Wantage, Oxfordshire OX12 8JY
Tel: 01235 821 821
Fax: 01235 821 155
Email: info@moonlightpublishing.co.uk
Website: www.moonlightpublishing.co.uk
Distributor: BookSource, 50 Cambuslang Road, Cambuslang,
Glasgow G32 8NB; Tel: 0845 370 0067; Fax: 0845 370 0068

The NATIONAL
ARCHIVES
of SCOTLAND

NATIONAL ARCHIVES OF SCOTLAND PS

The National Archives of Scotland preserves, protects and promotes the nation's records, and aims to make its holdings more accessible to all users. Our publications are designed to support this work. In addition to our own publications, some leading titles are published on our behalf by Birlinn Ltd, including the leading work *Tracing Your Scottish Ancestors*, now in its fifth edition.

Established: 1994
Publications (yearly average): 2
Types of books published: General historical and educational publications
Submission details: Unsolicited manuscripts are not accepted

CONTACTS
Department: Collections Development
Address: HM General Register House, 2 Princes Street, Edinburgh EH1 3YY
Tel: 0131 535 1353
Fax: 0131 535 1363
Email: publications@nas.gov.uk
Website: www.nas.gov.uk
Distributor: Collections Development Branch, National Archives of Scotland

NATIONAL GALLERIES OF SCOTLAND

NATIONAL GALLERIES OF SCOTLAND **PS**

NGS Publishing is an established fine art and photography publisher. Our aim is to publish books with the highest design and production values which reflect the diversity of the four galleries that constitute the National Galleries of Scotland. A range of titles is produced each year including exhibition catalogues and leaflets, as well as books and guides to the permanent collection.

Titles in print: 80
Submission details: NGS does not accept unsolicited manuscripts

CONTACTS
People: Janis Adams (Head of Publishing), Christine Thompson (Publishing Manager), Olivia Sheppard (Publishing Assistant), Ann Laidlaw (Administration)
Address: NGS Publishing, Gallery of Modern Art, Belford Road, Edinburgh EH4 3DR
Tel: 0131 624 6257/6261/6269
Fax: 0131 623 7135
Email: publications@nationalgalleries.org
Website: www.nationalgalleries.org
Distributor: Antique Collectors' Club

NATIONAL LIBRARY OF SCOTLAND PS

The National Library of Scotland publishes accessible and attractive books on a broad range of historical 'Scottish interest' subjects that reflect the diverse nature of our collections.

Recent titles have covered the history of golf, printing in Scotland, and the contents of the archive of influential publishing firm, John Murray. We also produce a range of posters, prints, facsimiles, stationary and gift items inspired by collection material on sale in our shop.

We often work in partnership with commercial publishers and welcome proposals for books produced 'in association' with us that draw on both the wealth of our collections and the knowledge of our expert curatorial staff.

Our collections of over 14 million items chronicle virtually every aspect of Scotland and Scots over the centuries and provide ample subject matter for books. Key collections include the Scottish Screen Archive, maps, music, literary and illustrated manuscripts, children's literature, art books, street literature and the popular press.

Being a Legal Deposit library, we are entitled to claim copies of every book published in the UK and Ireland.

Established: 1925
Publications (yearly average): 1
Types of books published: Books on a broad range of Scottish cultural themes; facsimiles; maps; literary and historical books (usually in collaboration with other publishers)
Submission details: We do not accept unsolicited manuscripts

CONTACTS
People: Julian Stone (Marketing and Communications Officer)
Address: George IV Bridge, Edinburgh EH1 1EW
Tel: 0131 623 3700
Fax: 0131 623 3701
Email: marketing@nls.uk
Website: www.nls.uk
Distributor: National Library of Scotland

NEIL WILSON PUBLISHING LTD PS

Neil Wilson Publishing is an award-winning independent concern based in Glasgow that publishes predominantly non-fiction with a Scottish flavour. We occasionally venture into Irish territory and our travel and outdoors publications are worldwide in nature. NWP has been shortlisted for the Boardman-Tasker Award for mountain literature on several occasions with an outright win in 2004 with Trevor Braham's *When The Alps Cast Their Spell*. The 11:9 fiction list was launched with SAC funding in 2000 and is still in print. NWP is not currently commissioning any more fiction.

Other award-winning writers with NWP are Donald Mackintosh, Catherine Brown, Jim Perrin, Roger Protz and Jim Murray.

Established: 1992
Publications (yearly average): 6 plus reprints
Types of books published: Whisky, food, cookery and drink, travel memoir, climbing and hillwalking, Scottish humour, biography, history, Irish interest and true crime
Submission details: By email only. Synopsis and sample text/illustrations.

CONTACTS
People: Neil Wilson (Publisher)
Address: G/2, 19 Netherton Avenue, Glasgow G13 1BQ
Tel: 0141 954 8007
Fax: 0560 150 4806
Email: info@nwp.co.uk
Website: www.nwp.co.uk
Distributor: BookSource, 50 Cambuslang Road, Cambuslang, Glasgow G32 8NB; Tel: 0845 370 0067; Fax: 0845 370 0068

NEW IONA PRESS PS

Since 1990 The New Iona Press has published a dozen mostly non-fiction books all relating directly to Mull and Iona. Subjects have ranged from marble or granite quarrying to botany and crofting life, from the Gaelic songs of a Mull bard to the artists and craftsmen who flourished on Iona. A few titles have reappeared in second editions and some provide a unique record, eg the story of the world-famous Mull Little Theatre. It's a tiny enterprise, run from home when time and enthusiasm permit. The name evokes the original 'Iona Press', set up in an island bothy in the 1880s to print finely decorated pamphlets on local lore to sell to visitors from the summer steamships.

Established: 1990
Publications (yearly average): Occasional
Types of books published: Local and natural history of the Hebridean islands of Iona and Mull
Submission details: Sorry, no unsolicited manuscripts

CONTACTS
People: Mairi MacArthur
Address: The Bungalow, Ardival, Strathpeffer, Ross-shire IV14 9DS
Tel/fax: 01997 421 186
Email: mairimacarthur@yahoo.co.uk
Distributor: Contact Mairi MacArthur or sales@bookspeed.com

National Museums Scotland

NMS ENTERPRISES LIMITED – PUBLISHING 🄿🅂

NMS Enterprises Limited – Publishing is the publishing division of National Museums Scotland.

We produce lavishly illustrated catalogues for Museum exhibitions such as, in 2008, *Silver: Made in Scotland*, celebrating 550 years of hallmarking in Scotland. Our list is very varied, with titles such as *Commando Country*; *Minerals of Scotland*; *Bagpipes: A National Collection of a National Instrument*; *Understanding Scottish Graveyards*; and *Weights and Measures in Scotland* (winner of the 2005 Saltire Society / National Library of Scotland Research Book of the Year Award); and the *Scotties* activity series for young readers.

Some of our books have been in print for many years, eg *The Scenery of Scotland* by WJ Baird has been selling since 1988; Hugh Cheape's *Tartan* was first published in 1991.

Most of our books come through Museum curators or are commissioned, but the Publishing Director is open to ideas of scholarly or popular Scottish interest in our subject areas.

Established: 1985 as National Museums of Scotland; 2002 as NMS Enterprises Limited – Publishing
Publications (yearly average): 12
Types of books published: Trade; scholarly books on history, art, archaeology, science, technology, geology, ethnography, natural history; popular Scottish history and culture; biography; photographic archive
Submission details: Send an outline and a covering letter in the first instance

CONTACTS
People: Lesley Taylor (Publishing Director), Kate Blackadder (Marketing and Publicity), Margaret Wilson (Administrator)
Address: NMS Enterprises Limited - Publishing, National Museums Scotland, Chambers Street, Edinburgh EH1 1JF
Tel: 0131 247 4026
Fax: 0131 247 4012
Email: publishing@nms.ac.uk
Website: www.nms.ac.uk/books
Distributors:
Scotland - BookSource, 50 Cambuslang Road, Cambuslang, Glasgow G32 8NB; Tel: 0845 370 0067; Fax: 0845 370 0068
USA: Woodstocker Books/Antique Collectors Club; Orders Tel (toll free): 845 679 4024; Fax: 845 679 4093; Email: woodstocker@woodstockerbooks.com

PERTH AND KINROSS COUNCIL LIBRARIES
AND LIFELONG LEARNING PS

Perth and Kinross Libraries have published around 30 books of local interest in recent years. There are details of how to order these on the website or many of them can be found in the Local Studies Section of AK Bell Library in Perth.

Established: 1988
Types of books published: Books of local interest; local authors; general

CONTACTS
People: Kenny McWilliam (Commercial Services Manager)
Address: AK Bell Library, York Place, Perth PH2 8EP
Tel: 01738 444 949
Fax: 01738 477 010
Email: library@pkc.gov.uk
Website: www.pkc.gov.uk/library
Distributor: AK Bell Library (Tel: 01738 444 949)

RIAS
The Royal Incorporation
of Architects in Scotland

RIAS PUBLISHING PS

We are dedicated to producing books that stimulate awareness of Scotland's built environment in an entertaining and informative way. Since 1982, inspired by our Charter's objective 'to foster the study of the national architecture of Scotland and to encourage its development', the RIAS has worked to publish guides for each major city and region of Scotland. Two-thirds of the series have now been published in a venture unmatched elsewhere in the world. The guides cover a wide spectrum of buildings from the earliest-known structures to projects still on the drawing-board and have proved to be a source of delight for readers everywhere. Over the years, our range of titles has strengthened to include other works of architectural merit such as monographs and reference books. RIAS Publishing is committed to promoting architecture in Scotland, and we will continue to find new and exciting ways to inspire appreciation of our national heritage.

The RIAS also has a specialist bookshop at 15 Rutland Square, Edinburgh which offers the country's widest range of architecture books, technical documents and building contracts.

Established: 1982 (previously RS Publications and The Rutland Press)
Publications (yearly average): 4
Types of books published: The Illustrated Architectural Guides to Scotland series, Architectural Reference and Monographs
Submission details: No unsolicited manuscripts accepted

CONTACTS
Address: 15 Rutland Square, Edinburgh EH1 2BE
Tel: 0131 229 7545
Fax: 0131 228 2188
Email: info@rias.org.uk
Website: www.rias.org.uk
Distributor: BookSource, 50 Cambuslang Road, Cambuslang, Glasgow G32 8NB; Tel: 0845 370 0067; Fax: 0845 370 0068; Representation: Seol Ltd

ROYAL BOTANIC GARDEN EDINBURGH PS

The Royal Botanic Garden Edinburgh (RBGE), founded in 1670, is a world renowned centre for plant research, conservation and education. Its four Gardens – the 'Botanics' in Edinburgh, Benmore in Argyll, Logan in Galloway and Dawyck in the Scottish Borders – grow more than 15,000 species between them. The Gardens are also popular visitor attractions offering fun and inspiring events for adults and children.

The RBGE Publications Office publishes visitor information as well as botanical journals, scientific reports, colour plant atlases and plant monographs.

Established: RBGE founded in 1670, publications office opened in 1986
Publications (yearly average): 10
Types of books published: Botanical, horticultural, scientific books
Submission details: Submit a book synopsis along with a book proposal outlining potential markets and 3 sample chapters

CONTACTS
People: Hamish Adamson (Publications Manager)
Address: 20a Inverleith Row, Edinburgh EH3 5LR
Tel (general): 0131 248 2819
Fax: 0131 248 2827
Email (general): pps@rbge.org.uk
Website: www.rbge.org.uk
Online book catalogue: www.rbge.org.uk/publications
Distributor: RBGE

RCAHMS

ROYAL COMMISSION ON THE ANCIENT
AND HISTORICAL MONUMENTS OF SCOTLAND PS

RCAHMS publications deliver wonderfully illustrated and immaculately researched titles to anyone with an interest in Scotland's history and built heritage.

One of Scotland's national collections, RCAHMS records, interprets and maintains information on the architectural, industrial, archaeological and maritime heritage of Scotland. This is an ongoing task as perceptions of the historic environment change, knowledge and research develops, and as landscapes and townscapes are built, demolished and radically altered.

The work is as essential today as it was when RCAHMS was founded in 1908. The accumulated results of 100 years of surveying, recording and collecting provides a fascinating picture of the human influence on the landscape of Scotland from earliest times to the present day. This information, which includes 15 million items of archive including photographs, maps, drawings and documents, is made widely available to the public in exhibitions, via the web or browsed in person at RCAHMS' premises in Edinburgh.

SCRAN, an online archive providing educational access to digital materials representing Scotland's culture and history, is now part of RCAHMS. The website (www.scran.ac.uk) contains 360,000 images, movies and sound clips from museums, galleries, archives and the media.

Established: 1908
Publications: 10
Types of books published: Both general trade and specialised books exploring the architecture, archaeology and industry of Scotland
Submission details: Do not accept unsolicited manuscripts

CONTACTS
People: Rebecca M Bailey (Head of Education and Outreach); James Crawford (Communications Officer); Neil Fraser (Scran Marketing Officer)
Address: John Sinclair House, 16 Bernard Terrace, Edinburgh EH8 9NX
Tel: 0131 662 1456
Fax: 0131 662 1477
Email: info@rcahms.gov.uk
Website: www.rcahms.gov.uk; www.scran.ac.uk
Distributor: BookSource, 50 Cambuslang Road, Cambuslang, Glasgow G32 8NB; Tel: 0845 370 0067; Fax: 0845 370 0068

SAINT ANDREW PRESS PS

Saint Andrew Press was founded in 1954 to publish the works of William Barclay. Since then, over 17 million copies of William Barclay's bible commentaries have been sold, and continue to sell around the world. Saint Andrew Press now publishes a broad range of titles catering to a wide, international readership, bringing titles that imaginatively help readers explore spirituality, faith, culture and ethical and moral issues in today's world.

Bestsellers include *Reformation*, journalist Harry Reid's magnum opus (published to coincide with the 500th anniversary of Calvin's birth) and the *Daily Study Bible Series* by William Barclay (over 17 million copies sold worldwide).

Forthcoming highlights include the new *Insights* series, a biography of George Mackay Brown by Ron Ferguson (including the letters between George and Stella – the muse of Rose Street), and *The Gospel According to Burns*.

Saint Andrew Press has merged with Scottish Christian Press and is now the sole publishing house of the Church of Scotland.

Established: 1954
Publications (yearly average): 40
Types of books published: High-quality titles for the Christian and general markets. Christian thought and worship, Scottish interest, history, biography. Titles with a wide religious or spiritual appeal that will meet the needs of readers with enquiring minds and an interest in thought-provoking writing.

CONTACTS
People: Ann Crawford (Head of Publishing); Richard Allen (Editorial Manager); Jonny Gallant (Sales and Marketing Manager); Christine Causer (Administrator)
Address: 121 George Street, Edinburgh EH2 4YN
Tel: 0131 225 5722 (ext 305)
Fax: 0131 240 2236
Email: standrewpress@cofscotland.org.uk
Website: www.churchofscotland.org.uk/standrewpress
Distributor: Marston Book Services Ltd, PO Box 269, Abingdon, Oxfordshire OX14 4SD; Tel: 01235 465 579

SALTIRE
SOCIETY

THE SALTIRE SOCIETY PS

The Saltire Society was founded in 1936 at a time, to quote Edwin Muir, when Scotland seemed to many people to be 'falling apart because there was no force to hold it together'. The aim of the Society was to counter this risk. It proposed to increase awareness of the Scottish cultural heritage, enhance our contribution to the arts and sciences, and 'advance Scotland's standing as a vibrant, creative force in European civilisation'. We have pursued these objectives by many means. They include campaigns, conferences, performances, publications, and a wide range of award schemes. We have been assisted by many individuals and organisations and there is no doubt that the cultural atmosphere of Scotland has been radically transformed in these last seventy years. We publish a few books each year on diverse aspects of Scottish life and letters, including history, literature, ideas and the Scots and Gaelic languages.

Established: 1936
Publications (yearly average): 2
Types of books published: Scottish and Gaelic interest; history; current affairs; criticism; biography
Submission details: 2 chapters of any relevant completed manuscript

CONTACTS
People: Ian Scott (Editorial) and Paul Scott (Committee Convener), both c/o Saltire Society, Address: 9 Fountain Close, 22 High Street, Edinburgh EH1 1TF. Seol Ltd (Marketing, Sales), West Newington House, 10 Newington Road, Edinburgh EH9 1QS. Tel: 0131 668 1458.
Address: 9 Fountain Close, 22 High Street, Edinburgh EH1 1TF
Tel: 0131 556 1836
Fax: 0131 557 1675
Email: saltire@saltiresociety.org.uk
Website: www.saltiresociety.org.uk
Distributor: BookSource, 50 Cambuslang Road, Cambuslang, Glasgow G32 8NB; Tel: 0845 370 0067; Fax: 0845 370 0068

SANDSTONE PRESS LTD PS

Sandstone Press is a publisher of non-fiction and fiction books. Based in the Highlands of Scotland, the company is characterised by high editorial and design standards, internationalism, and a strong engagement with the contemporary world using modern methods.

Sandstone Press books have been shortlisted for many literary awards including the Saltire Society Awards, Scottish Arts Council Awards and Boardman Tasker Award. The company is also active in Gaelic education, developing a new kind of fiction reader for advanced learners.

At the beginning of 2010 the company placed general fiction beside its already highly developed non-fiction list and now publishes humour, crime, family, drama, outdoor, literary and travel books.

The website www.sandstonepress.com is an important part of the company's publishing output with many authors contributing regularly to their own blogspots, a Home Page twitter feed, and regularly edited News.

Established: 2002
Publications (yearly): 10–20
Types of book published: Non-fiction and adult literacy in both English and Gaelic
Submissions: See the website: www.sandstonepress.com

CONTACTS
People: Robert Davidson (Managing Director); Moira Forsyth (Submissions Director); Iain Gordon (Director and Company Secretary)
Address: PO Box 5725, One High Street, Dingwall, Ross-shire, IV15 9WJ
Tel: 01349 862 583
Fax: 01349 862 583
Email (general): info@sandstonepress.com
Website: www.sandstonepress.com
Distributor: BookSource, 50 Cambuslang Road, Cambuslang, Glasgow G32 8NB; Tel: 0845 370 0067; Fax: 0845 370 0068

SARABAND PS

Saraband publishes well-written and beautifully produced illustrated non-fiction titles in subject areas including the arts, architecture, history, the environment, reference and mind/body/spirit, for a general audience. In 2009 we were delighted to have had two of our titles featured as Books From Scotland's Book of the Month: the delightful, Scottish best-selling *The Garden Cottage Diaries – My Year in the Eighteenth Century*, by Fiona J Houston; and *Scottish Ballet: Forty Years*, the anniversary celebration of our national ballet company by leading dance critic Mary Brennan, with stunning images by a number of prominent photographers.

Other recent titles include a fascinating exploration of life in Ancient Egypt through the art and artefacts and what we can learn from their symbolism (*The Hidden Life of Ancient Egypt*, by Clare Gibson); *The Sky Handbook*, by John Watson, published for the International Year of Astronomy; and a lavishly produced, critically acclaimed retrospective of the architect Frank Lloyd Wright, *The Wright Experience*, introduced by the Curator of the Frank Lloyd Wright Foundation.

Our captivating and attractive books have been published in many languages in Asia, Europe and the Americas. Founded in the USA in the early 1990s, we are international in outlook and often prepare co-editions with publishers around the world. Having relocated to Glasgow in 2000, we have recently published a selection of titles whose focus is closer to home.

Established: 2000
Publications (yearly average): 6
Types of books published: Illustrated non-fiction
Submission details: Do not accept unsolicited manuscripts

CONTACTS
People: Sara Hunt (Managing Director)
Address: Suite 202, 98 Woodlands Rd, Glasgow G3 6HB
Tel: 0141 337 2411
Fax: 0141 332 1863
Email: hermes@saraband.net
Website: www.saraband.net
Distributor: Please refer to the website above for distributor details

SCOTTISH BOOK TRUST PS

Scottish Book Trust is the leading agency for the promotion of literature in Scotland, developing innovative projects to encourage adults and children to read, write and be inspired by books.

Scottish Book Trust funds literature events connecting readers with writers, champions and supports Scottish writers and illustrators, runs the biggest children's book award in the UK (judged by thousands of children) and supports hundreds of teachers and librarians to help improve literacy. It also runs an early years programme including bookgifting to every child in Scotland.

Its website has a wealth of valuable resources about reading and creative writing for both adults and children, including searchable databases of authors and books. The website also has full details of all projects and how to get involved.

Company established: 1961

CONTACTS
People: Marc Lambert (Chief Executive); Jeanette Harris (General Manager); Sophie Moxon (Head of Programme); Marion Bourbouze (Head of Marketing & Audience Development); Michael Merillo (Venue Manager); Julia Collins (Finance Manager); Olivier Joly (Press Officer)
Address: Sandeman House, Trunk's Close, 55 High Street, Edinburgh EH1 1SR
Tel: 0131 524 0160
Fax: 0131 524 0161
Email: info@scottishbooktrust.com
Website: www.scottishbooktrust.com

SCOTTISH NATURAL HERITAGE PS

The role of Scottish Natural Heritage is to look after the natural heritage, help people to enjoy and value it, and encourage people to use it sustainably. In fulfilling this role, Scottish Natural Heritage produces a wide range of publications ranging from books and magazines to leaflets and calendars as well as strategy and other policy documents. They currently have over 500 titles.

Established: 1992
Types of books published: Environment; natural heritage; government and education
Submission details: Unsolicited manuscripts are not accepted

CONTACTS
People: Pam Malcolm (Publications Officer), based at the Aberdeen office, 17 Rubislaw Terrace, Aberdeen AB10 1XE
Address: Scottish Natural Heritage, Battleby, Redgorton, Perth PH1 3EW
Tel: 01738 458 530/01224 654 330
Fax: 01738 827 411/01224 630 250
Email: pam.malcolm@snh.gov.uk
Website: www.snh.org.uk
Distributor: Scottish Natural Heritage, Battleby, Redgorton, Perth;
Tel: 01738 458530

SCOTTISH TEXT SOCIETY PS

The Scottish Text Society is the leading publisher of older Scots literature. Since its foundation the Society has played a significant part in reviving interest in the literature and languages of Scotland. It has published around 150 volumes covering poetry, drama and prose from the fourteenth to the nineteenth centuries, each of which combines scholarship and accessibility. Texts currently available include reprints of the Society's editions of the great epic poems of the Wars of Independence, *Barbour's Bruce* and *Hary's Wallace*; a revised edition of *The Shorter Poems of Gavin Douglas*; an edition of the poetry of Scotland's greatest Renaissance poet, *Alexander Montgomerie, Poems*; and Sir David Hume's *History of the House of Angus*. In 2008 the Society published editions of important late-medieval poetry, *The Poems of Walter Kennedy* and *Golagros and Gawane*. In collaboration with the National Library of Scotland it has also issued a DVD, *The Chepman and Myllar Prints*, which gives access, via digitised facsimile, to the work of Scotland's first printers.

Established: 1882
Publications (yearly average): 1
Types of books published: Editions of Scottish texts, chiefly of the medieval and Renaissance periods and including works of historiography, theology and imaginative literature
Submission details: Potential editors should send an outline of the proposed edition to the secretary, for submission to the council. Guidelines for Editors and a proforma for proposal submissions can be found on the Society's website

CONTACTS
People: Dr N Royan (Editorial Secretary), School of English Studies, University of Nottingham, University Park, Nottingham NG7 2RD
Address: The main contact is Dr N Royan above. The Society's institutional address is: Scottish Text Society, 25 Buccleuch Place, Edinburgh, EH8 9LN
Email: editorialsecretary@scottishtextsociety.org; membershipsecretary@scottishtextsociety.org
Website: www.scottishtextsociety.org
Distributor: Boydell & Brewer Ltd, PO Box 9, Woodbridge, Suffolk IP12 3DF; Tel: 01394 610 600; Fax: 01394 610 316

SERAFINA PRESS PS

Based at the Smokehouse Gallery, in the Borders seaside town of Eyemouth, Serafina Press aims to produce art-driven children's picture books. The books have a strong sense of their Borders location, but are not limited in appeal to the region – they sell around the UK, and abroad. The stories are aimed at children up to eight years, with illustrations on every page. Cards featuring some of the characters are available.

Serafina Press has a particular interest in working with young illustrators, and has worked with a final-year student and a recent graduate from Edinburgh College of Art.

The Mouse of Gold has been translated into Arabic in 2009, with the first edition selling out within a week, and further Arabic editions are planned.

Established: 2006
Types of books published: Children's full colour picture books
Submission details: We have a very limited list, and several new titles planned, so we're not looking for story ideas for 2010. Illustrators are welcome to send samples of work for consideration for future projects.

CONTACTS
People: Jennifer Doherty (Owner)
Address: The Smokehouse Gallery, St Ellas Place, Eyemouth TD14 5HP
Tel: 07906 064 982, 01890 752 116
Email: info@serafinapress.co.uk
Website: www.serafinapress.co.uk
Distributor: Bookspeed, 16 Salamander Yards, Edinburgh EH Tel: 0131 467 8100 Fax: 0131 467 8008 sales@bookspeed.com or order directly on 01890 752 116.

sportscotland

SPORTSCOTLAND PS

sportscotland is the national agency for sport. Our aim is to increase participation and improve performance by investing in and joining up the people, places and thinking that make sport happen.

We work with partners to build success for Scottish sport. We advise the Scottish Government and support the delivery of its policies; we lead, support and coordinate the key providers of sport; and we invest National Lottery and Scottish Government funding.

We also deliver quality services in targeted area through the **sport**scotland institute of sport and our three national training centres.

In everything we do we aspire to act in the best interests of Scottish sport – putting sport first.

Established: 1972 (formerly Scottish Sports Council)
Types of books published: Sport strategy documents; sport research and governing body information

CONTACTS
People: Communications Team
Address: Doges, Templeton on the Green, 62 Templeton Street, Glasgow G40 1DA
Tel: 0141 534 6500
Fax: 0141 534 6501
Email: library@sportscotland.org.uk
Website: www.sportscotland.org.uk
Distributor: sportscotland

STRIDENT PUBLISHING PS

Strident Publishing is a dynamic publisher of fiction. Most of our list is for those of school age; however, we also publish a few crossover titles (e.g. *Bad Faith* by Gillian Philip) that are read by teenagers and adults alike.

Strident produces books with a bit of spark – books that give people a kick out of reading. They are bold and modern and cry out to be read and discussed. We are renowned for working extremely hard to market our titles.

Our list includes titles by award-winning and shortlisted authors including Catherine MacPhail (*Granny Nothing*), DA Nelson (*DarkIsle*), Linda Strachan (*Spider*), Keith Charters (*Lee and the Consul Mutants*), Paul Biegel (*The King of the Copper Mountains*) and Gillian Philip (*Bad Faith*).

Established: 2005
Types of books published: Fiction for children of school age, young adults and adult/young adult crossover. No non-fiction.
Submission details: Send blurb plus first three chapters, ideally by email

CONTACTS
People: Keith Charters (Managing Director), Graham Watson (Editor), Alison Stroak (Marketing), Sallie Moffat (Design and Editorial)
Address: 22 Strathwhillan Drive, Hairmyres, East Kilbride, G75 8GT
Tel: 01355 220 588
Email: info@stridentpublishing.co.uk
Website: www.stridentpublishing.co.uk
Distributor: BookSource, 50 Cambuslang Road, Cambuslang, Glasgow G32 8NB; Tel: 0845 370 0067; Fax: 0845 370 0068

ULSTER HISTORICAL FOUNDATION PS

Over the last 40 years the Ulster Historical Foundation has established itself as one of the leading publishers in its field. The Foundation focuses primarily on high quality Irish history and genealogy books for general readership, including an exclusive range of luxury hardback titles. We specialise in local and family history texts, along with genealogical guides for family historians seeking to trace their Irish or Scots-Irish roots.

The Foundation also publishes a number of texts for the academic market, including the prestigious six-volume History of the Irish Parliament. We produce Irish political, economic and social, industrial and local histories, aimed primarily at university students and academics. However, we have also published several educational history titles for children, which have been designed to support the national curriculum.

Established: 1956
Publications (yearly average): 6
Types of books published: Irish and Ulster history and local history, genealogy, academic and educational, non-fiction, historical reference
Submission details: Sample chapter, synopsis of text, chapter titles and short description, bibliography

CONTACTS
People: Fintan Mullan (Executive Director), Kathryn McKelvey (Office Manager), Kate Tumilty (Publications Officer)
Address: 49 Malone Road, Belfast, BT9 6RY
Tel: 028 9066 1988
Fax: 028 9066 1977
Email: enquiry@uhf.org.uk
Website: www.ancestryireland.com; www.booksireland.org.uk
Distributor: Contact Ulster Historical Foundation

VAGABOND VOICES PS

Vagabond Voices is principally a publisher of translated novels and Scottish literary works. Although based on the Isle of Lewis, a 'remote', north-western corner of our continent, it is fervently European in its aims. Moreover, it sees no contradiction between its geographical location and its cosmopolitan vocation.

Vagabond Voices does not want to make great claims for its own output – it is for others to make their judgements – but it most certainly can say that it will bring an element of variety to our increasingly conformist publishing world. We look for works of literary worth, of course, but we are also interested in presenting unusual texts and different ways of doing things to the English-speaking world and indeed to other writers, particularly here in Scotland. A vibrant culture is always a balance between being true to one's own traditions and open to and curious about those of others. Within the restrictions imposed by our limited resources, we hope to make a small contribution in that direction.

Information on our books, authors and future plans can be found on our website: www.vagabondvoices.co.uk

Established: December 2008
Books published per year: 5-10
Types of books published: Literary fiction, non-fiction, poetry and polemics (much of the overall output will be in translation)
Submissions: See website – www.vagabondvoices.co.uk

CONTACTS
People: Allan Cameron (sole director), Margaret MacKelvie (sales and marketing), Janice Brent (copyediting and editorial assistance)
Address: 3 Sulaisiadar, An Rudha, Isle of Lewis, HS2 0PU
Tel: 01851 870 050
Email: sales@vagabondvoices.co.uk
Website: www.vagabondvoices.co.uk
Orders through: Gardners or Vagabond Voices

WEST DUNBARTONSHIRE LIBRARIES PS

As part of its commitment to literature and culture in its area, West Dunbartonshire Libraries publish books with a local history context. The two most recent publications have been: *Changing Identities Ancient Roots* edited by Ian Brown (the story of three distinct but interconnected communities) and *A Close Community: Life in an Alexandria Tenement* by Malcolm Lobban. However, far and away the most successful publication has been *Ships for a Nation* by Ian Johnston (published in 2001 and still selling well to date).

West Dunbartonshire Libraries also run numerous literary events of which the highlight is the annual book festival 'Booked!' now in its tenth year. Among the guests at the 2009 festival were Tom Devine (who delivered the prestigious Alistair Pearson Lecture), Louise Welsh, Iain Banks and Denise Mina, as well as a range of children's authors including David Lucas, Catherine Forde, The Two Steves, and Julia Donaldson.

Established: 1996 (at local government re-organisation)
Types of books published: Local interest

CONTACTS
People: Ian Baillie (01389 772 161)
Address: 19 Poplar Road, Dumbarton G82 2RJ
Tel: 01389 608 045
Fax: 01389 608 044
Email: ian.baillie@west-dunbarton.gov.uk
Website: www.west-dunbarton.gov.uk
Distributor: West Dunbartonshire Libraries and Cultural Services

WHITTLES PUBLISHING PS

Whittles Publishing has expanded significantly over recent years, to become a well-known technical publisher on the global stage with authors of international standing. Consolidation of our lists in geomatics, civil/structural engineering and fuel and energy science has now been accompanied by a new list in materials and manufacturing, including nanotechnology.

We are also known for our quality general list which includes landscape/nature writing and maritime books with authors such as Roy Dennis, Hamish Brown, Mike Tomkies and Chris Foote Wood. We take pride in publishing well-produced and attractive books which are a pleasure to read.

Following the acquisition of the autobiography of Sir Gulam Noon who was embroiled in the 'cash for honours' scandal, we are now adding other books to our Asian Connections list. As well as distributing Talisman Books (Singapore) in Europe, Middle East and Africa, other new titles include *The Making of India, a story of British enterprise* by Kartar Lalvani and Peter English, and *Woman – Acceptable Exploitation for Profit*, a powerful book by Baroness Shreela Flather that offers a new solution in the fight against poverty and hunger in the developing countries.

Established: 1986
Publications (yearly average): 25
Types of books published: Civil and structural engineering; geomatics; geotechnics; manufacturing and materials technology including nanotechnology; fuel and energy science; nature writing/landscape; maritime; pharology; military history; classic fiction
Submission details: Please contact Dr Keith Whittles with brief synopsis and sample writing

CONTACTS
People: Dr Keith Whittles (Editorial, Sales), Mrs Sue Steven (Sales and Promotion)
Address: Dunbeath, Caithness KW6 6EY
Tel: 01593 731 333
Fax: 01593 731 400
Email: info@whittlespublishing.com
Website: www.whittlespublishing.com
Distributor: BookSource, 50 Cambuslang Road, Cambuslang, Glasgow G32 8NB; Tel: 0845 370 0067; Fax: 0845 370 0068

WITHERBY SEAMANSHIP INTERNATIONAL LTD PS

Witherby Seamanship International Ltd was established in 2008 through a merger between Witherbys Publishing and Seamanship International Ltd. The Witherby business dates back to 1740 when Thomas Witherby opened a stationery shop in Birchin Lane, London, next to the Sword Blade Coffee house, providing stationery and printing for the newly founded commercial marine insurance market.

Established: 2008
Types of books published: Specialist publisher of marine training, reference and regulatory materials, providing books and publications to the shipping, marine and general insurance and legal industries
Submission details: Send a synopsis of a sample chapter, a CV and supporting information. Please send submissions by email or by post – contact details below.

CONTACTS
People: Iain Macneil (Managing Director); Kat Heathcote (Editorial Director); Stewart Heney (General Manager); Clare Barron (Sales & Marketing, Marine); Christine Rogers (Sales & Marketing, Insurance & Legal)
Address: 4 Dunlop Square, Livingston EH54 8SB
Tel: 01506 463 227
Fax: 01506 468 999
Email: info@emailws.com
Website: www.witherbyseamanship.com

List of Publishers in Scotland

There is no definitive list of all publishers in Scotland. We have aimed to include as many publishers as possible in this list though we have excluded self-publishers, vanity publishers and companies that produce only promotional materials where we have been able to identify them. Members of Publishing Scotland are denoted by the key **PS** and there is more information about them on pages 19–81.

ACADEMY MEDIA **PS**
Academy Media, Firth View, Gower Street, Brora KW9 6PU
T: 01408 622 183; **E:** info@academymedia.com; **W:** www.academymedia.com
DVD biographies and programmes about history, literature, music and languages

ACAIR LTD **PS**
7 James Street, Stornoway, Isle of Lewis HS1 2QN
T: 01851 703 020; **F:** 01851 703 294; **E:** info@acairbooks.com;
W: www.acairbooks.com
Gaelic books mainly for children

ALLAN (R L) & SON PUBLISHERS
Unit J, 47 Purdon Street, Glasgow G11 6AF
T: 0141 337 6529; **E:** info@bibles-direct.com; **W:** www.bibles-direct.com
English-language editions of the Bible

ARGYLL PUBLISHING
Glendaruel, Argyll PA22 3AE
T: 01369 820 229; **F:** 01369 820 372; **W:** www.argyllbookstore.co.uk
Scottish Review of Books, Scottish interest

ASSOCIATION FOR SCOTTISH LITERARY STUDIES **PS**
c/o Dept of Scottish History, University of Glasgow, 7 University Gardens, Glasgow G12 8QH
T: 0141 330 5309; **E:** office@asls.org.uk; **W:** www.asls.org.uk
Scottish literature, anthologies of new Scottish writing

ATELIER BOOKS **PS**
6 Dundas Street, Edinburgh EH3 6HZ
T: 0131 557 4050; **E:** art@bournefineart.com; **W:** www.bournefineart.com
Art and artists

AVIZANDUM PUBLISHING LTD
58 Candlemaker Row, Edinburgh EH1 2QE
T: 0131 220 3373; **E**: margaret@avizandum.com; **W**: www.avizandum.com
Law

BARRINGTON STOKE LTD **PS**
18 Walker Street, Edinburgh EH3 6HZ
T: 0131 225 4113; **F**: 0131 225 4140; **E**: info@barringtonstoke.co.uk;
W: www.barringtonstoke.co.uk
Children's fiction for dyslexic, struggling and reluctant readers

BENCHMARK BOOKS
50 Shuna Place, Newton Mearns, Glasgow G77 6TN
T: 0141 639 0154; **E**: enquiries@benchmarkbooks.co.uk;
W: www.benchmarkbooks.co.uk
Children's football books

BILL LAWSON PUBLICATIONS
The Old Schoolhouse, Taobh Tuath, (Northton), Isle of Harris HS3 3JA
T: 01859 520 488; **F**: 01859 520 488; **E**: lawsonbil@aol.com;
W: www.billlawson.com
Genealogy research material for the Outer Hebrides

BIRLINN LTD
(incorporating House of Lochar, John Donald, Mercat Press and Polygon)
West Newington House, 10 Newington Road, Edinburgh EH9 1QS
T: 0131 668 4371; **F**: 0131 668 4466; **E**: info@birlinn.co.uk; **W**: www.birlinn.co.uk
Scottish fiction and non-fiction

BLACK & WHITE PUBLISHING **PS**
29 Ocean Drive, Leith, Edinburgh EH6 6JL
T: 0131 625 4500; **F**: 0131 625 4501; **E**: mail@blackandwhitepublishing.com;
W: www.blackandwhitepublishing.com
Scottish literature, biographies, history

BLACKWELL PUBLISHING LTD
101 George Street, Edinburgh EH2 3ES
T: 0131 226 7232; **F**: 0131 226 3803; **W**: www.blackwellpublishing.com
Academic journals, books and online content

BLOOMSBURY PROFESSIONAL
9/10 St Andrews Square, Edinburgh EH2 2AF
T: 0131 718 6073; **F:** 0131 718 6100;
E: customerservices@bloomsburyprofessional.com;
W: www.bloomsburyprofessional.com
Books and information services for lawyers, accountants and business people

BOOKS NOIR
22 Church Road, Giffnock, Glasgow G46 6LT
T: 0141 571 3963; **F:** 0141 571 5684; **E:** info@booksnoir.com;
W: www.booksnoir.com
Children's adventure, crime and detective stories

BRAE EDITIONS
Buckquoy, Finstown, Orkney KW17 2JS
T: 01856 761508; **E:** info@braeprojects.com; **W:**http://braeprojects.com/shopsite/
Poetry and non-fiction

BRIGHT RED PUBLISHING `PS`
6 Stafford Street, Edinburgh EH3 7AU
T: 0131 220 5804; **F:** 0131 220 6710; **E:** info@brightredpublishing.co.uk;
W: www.brightredpublishing.co.uk
Scottish secondary educational publishing

BROWN & WHITTAKER PUBLISHING `PS`
Tobermory, Isle of Mull PA75 6PR
T: 01688 302 381; **E:** olivebrown@msn.com; **W:** www.brown-whittaker.co.uk
Isle of Mull history, archaeology, history, wildlife, genealogy and walking guides

BROWN, SON & FERGUSON `PS`
4–10 Darnley Street, Glasgow G41 2SD
T: 0141 429 1234; **F:** 0141 420 1694; **E:** info@skipper.co.uk; **W:** www.skipper.co.uk
Nautical and plays

CANONGATE BOOKS `PS`
14 High Street, Edinburgh EH1 1TE
T: 0131 557 5111; **F:** 0131 557 5211; **E:** info@canongate.co.uk;
W: www.canongate.net
Fiction, biography and general non-fiction

CAPERCAILLIE BOOKS
1–3 St Colme Street, Edinburgh EH3 6AA
T: 0131 220 8310; **F:** 0131 220 8201; **E:** info@capercailliebooks.co.uk;
W: www.capercailliebooks.co.uk; www.fairplaypress.co.uk
Non-fiction (and drama: Fairplay Press)

CARRICK MEDIA
32 Briar Grove, Ayr, Ayrshire KA7 3PD
T: 01292 283 337; **F:** 01292 283 337; **E:** carrickmedia@btinternet.com;
W: www.whoswhoinscotland.com
Publishers of Who's Who in Scotland

CHAPMAN PUBLISHING PS
4 Broughton Place, Edinburgh EH1 3RX
T: 0131 557 2207; **E:** chapman-pub@blueyonder.co.uk;
W: www.chapman-pub.co.uk
Chapman journal, poetry and new writing

CHARLES TAIT PHOTOGRAPHIC
Kelton, Old Finstown Road, Kirkwall, Orkney KW15 1TR
T: 01856 873 738; **F:** 01856 875 313; **E:** charles.tait@zetnet.co.uk;
W: www.charles-tait.co.uk
Photographic

CHRISTIAN FOCUS PUBLICATIONS LTD
Geanies House, Fearn, Tain, Ross-shire IV20 1TW
T: 01862 871 011; **F:** 01862 871 699; **E:** info@christianfocus.com;
W: www.christianfocus.com
Christian titles for adults and children

CLAN BOOKS
Clandon House, The Cross, Doune, Perthshire FK16 6BE
T: 01786 841330; **F:** 01786 841 326; **E:** clanbooks@intertrade1.net;
W: www.walkingscotlandseries.co.uk
Scottish walking guides

CONTINUING EDUCATION GATEWAY PS
199 Nithsdale Road, Glasgow G41 5EX
T: 0141 422 1070; **F**: 0141 422 2919; **E**: ceg@ceg.org.uk; **W**: www.ceg.org.uk
Careers and educational information books and leaflets

COMHAIRLE NAN LEABHRAICHEAN (THE GAELIC BOOKS COUNCIL) PS
22 Mansfield Street, Glasgow G11 5QP
T: 0141 337 6211; **E**: brath@gaelicbooks.org;
W: www.gaelicbooks.org; www.ur-sgeul.com
Catalogues, Gaelic book news magazines

CUALANN PRESS
6 Corpath Drive, Dunfermline, Fife KY12 7XG
T/F: 01383 733 724; **E**: info@cualann.com **W**: www.cualann.com
Historical and outdoor

D C THOMSON
80 Kingsway East, Dundee DD4 8SL
T: 01382 223 131; **F**: 01382 462 097; **W**: www.dcthomson.co.uk
Magazines, comics, newspapers, serials and journals

DIONYSIA PRESS PS
127 Milton Road West, 7 Duddingston House Courtyard, Edinburgh EH15 1JG
F: 0131 656 9565; **W**: http://wordpress.com/tag/dionysia-press
Greek poetry collections, plays, novels and translations

DENBURN BOOKS
49 Waverley Place, Aberdeen AB10 1XP
T: 01224 644 492
Aberdeenshire local history

DUDU NSOMBA PUBLICATIONS PS
5c Greystone Avenue, Rutherglen, Glasgow G73 3SN
T: 0141 647 5195; **E**: lwanda2000@yahoo.co.uk; **W**: www.pamtondo.com
Malawi and Africa: politics, literature, economics, music, novels, poetry, short stories and religion

DUNDEE CITY COUNCIL LEISURE AND COMMUNITIES
DEPARTMENT AND EDUCATION DEPARTMENT **PS**
The Wellgate, Dundee DD1 1DB
T: 01382 431 546; 01382 434 888; **E**: stuart.syme@dundeecity.gov.uk; moira.
foster@dundeecity.gov.uk; **W**: www.dundeecity.gov.uk/library
Education and local history

DUNDEE UNIVERSITY PRESS LTD
Tower Building, University of Dundee, Dundee DD1 4HN
T: 01382 384 413; **F**: 01382 229 948; **E**: dup@dundee.ac.uk;
W: www.dup.dundee.ac.uk
Law, history, energy, pathology, science and the professions

DUNEDIN ACADEMIC PRESS **PS**
Hudson House, 8 Albany Street, Edinburgh EH1 3QB
T: 0131 473 2397; **F**: 01250 870 920; **E**: mail@dunedinacademicpress.co.uk;
W: www.dunedinacademicpress.co.uk
Earth sciences, social sciences, humanities, history, Gaelic studies, and vocal studies

EAST LOTHIAN LIBRARY SERVICE **PS**
Library Headquarters, Dunbar Road, Haddington EH41 3PJ
T: 01620 828 200; 01620 828 201; **E**: smillar@eastlothiangov.uk;
W: www.eastlothian.gov.uk
Local publications including East Lothian 1945–2000 in 7 volumes

EDINBURGH UNIVERSITY PRESS **PS**
22 George Square, Edinburgh EH8 9LF
T: 0131 650 4218; **F**: 0131 662 3286;
E: editorial@eup.ed.ac.uk; marketing@eup.ed.ac.uk;
W: www.euppublishing.com
History, literature, linguistics and general academic titles, social sciences and humanities

EDPAX INTERNATIONAL LTD
Ayrshire Innovation Centre, 2 Cockburn Place, Riverside Business Park,
Irvine KA11 5DA
T: 01294 316 519; **F**: 01294 316 553; **E**: info@edpax.com; **W**: www.edpax.com
Interactive whiteboard software and books for primary schools

ELSEVIER LTD
London House, 20–22 East London Street, Edinburgh EH7 4BQ
T: 0131 524 1700; **F:** 0131 524 1800; **W:** www.elsevier.com
Health sciences, medicine, science and technology

THE ERNEST PRESS
17 Carleton Drive, Glasgow G46 6AQ
T/F: 0141 637 5492; **E:** sales@ernest-press.co.uk; **W:** www.ernest-press.co.uk
Mountain and outdoors literature

FIDRA BOOKS LTD `PS`
219 Bruntsfield Place, Edinburgh EH10 4DH
T: 0131 447 1917; **E:** info@fidrabooks.com; **W:** www.fidrabooks.com
Children's fiction

FINDHORN PRESS
305a The Park, Forres IV36 3TE
T: 01309 690 582; **F:** 01309 690 036; **E:** info@findhornpress.com;
W: www.findhornpress.com
Spirituality, healing and self development

FLEDGLING PRESS LTD `PS`
7 Lennox Street, Edinburgh EH4 1QB
T: 0131 332 6994; **E:** zander@fledglingpress.co.uk; **W:** www.fledglingpress.co.uk
Novels, human interest

FLORIS BOOKS `PS`
15 Harrison Gardens, Edinburgh EH11 1SH
T: 0131 337 2372; **F:** 0131 347 9919; **E:** floris@florisbooks.co.uk;
W: www.florisbooks.co.uk
Celtic; mind, body and spirit; children's; craft and activity

FORESTRY COMMISSION `PS`
231 Corstorphine Road, Edinburgh EH12 7AT
T: 0131 334 0303
E: elaine.dick@forestry.gsi.gov.uk
W: www.forestry.gov.uk/publications
Books on forest management, sustainable forestry, statistics etc

FORT PUBLISHING LTD
Old Belmont House, 12 Robsland Avenue, Ayr KA7 2RW
T: 01292 880 693; **F**: 01292 270 134
E: fortpublishing@aol.com
W: www.fortpublishing.co.uk
Crime, sport, history, local interest

GAELIC BOOKS COUNCIL, see *COMHAIRLE NAN LEABHRAICHEAN*

GEDDES & GROSSET `PS`
(and Waverley Books imprint)
144 Port Dundas Road, Glasgow G4 0HZ
T: 0141 567 2830; **F**: 0141 567 2831; **E**: info@gandg.sol.co.uk; info@waverley-books.co.uk; **W**: www.geddesandgrosset.co.uk; www.waverley-books.co.uk
Reference books, children's books, regional interest books and books as premiums and incentives

GLASGOW CITY LIBRARIES PUBLICATIONS `PS`
The Mitchell Library, North Street, Glasgow G3 7DN
T: 0141 287 2809; **E**: maureen.wilbraham@cls.glasgow.gov.uk;
W: www.glasgow.gov.uk
Glasgow interest

GLASGOW MUSEUMS PUBLISHING `PS`
Culture and Sport Glasgow, Glasgow Museums Resource Centre, 200 Woodhead Road, Glasgow G53 7NN
T: 0141 276 9452; **E**: susan.pacitti@cs.glasgow.gov.uk; **W**: www.glasgowmuseums.com
Art and artists, guidebooks to collections

GLEN MURRAY PUBLISHING
(incorporating Glen Murray, Galloway and Scottish Maritime Publishing)
8 Castle Street, Kirkcudbright, Dumfries and Galloway DG6 4JA
T: 05601 141 603; **E**: info@glenmurraypublishing.co.uk;
W: www.glenmurraypublishing.co.uk
Galloway, Scottish and maritime interest

THE GLENEIL PRESS PS
Whittingehame Mains, East Lothian EH41 4QA
T: 01620 860 292; **E:** gleneilpress@tiscali.co.uk; **W:** www.gleneil.com
Scottish history, biography and sporting

GOBLINSHEAD PS
130b Inveresk Road, Musselburgh EH21 7AY
T: 0131 665 2894; **F:** 0131 653 6566; **E:** goblinshead@sol.co.uk
Scottish history and travel guides

GRACE NOTE PUBLICATIONS PS
Grange of Locherlour, Ochtertyre, by Crieff, Perthshire PH7 4JS
T: 01764 655 979; **E:** books@gracenotereading.co.uk
Scottish history and travel guides

W GREEN
21 Alva Street, Edinburgh EH2 4PS
T: 0131 225 4879; **F:** 0131 225 2104; **E:** wgreen.enquiries@thomson.com;
W: www.wgreen.co.uk
Law

THE GRIMSAY PRESS
(also publishes as Zeticula, humming earth, Kennedy & Boyd,
Mansion Field and Covenanters Press)
57 St Vincent Crescent, Glasgow G3 8NQ
E: admin@thegrimsaypress.co.uk; **W:** www.thegrimsaypress.co.uk
Local, family and social history

HACHETTE SCOTLAND PS
2a Christie Street, Paisley PA1 1NB
T: 0141 552 8082; **E:** bob.mcdevitt@hachettescotland.co.uk
General fiction and non-fiction

HALLEWELL PUBLICATIONS PS
The Milton, Foss, Pitlochry, Perthshire PH16 5NQ
T: 01882 634 254; **E:** hallewell-pubs@btconnect.com; **W:** www.pocketwalks.com
Walking guides

HANDSEL PRESS
62 Toll Road, Kincardine, by Alloa FK10 4QZ
T: 01259 730 538; **W**: www.handselpress.co.uk
Christianity, and Christianity and the arts

HARDIE PRESS
35 Mountcastle Terrace, Edinburgh EH8 7SF
T: 0131 657 2097; **W**: www.hardiepress.co.uk
Music

HARPERCOLLINS PUBLISHERS 🅿🅢
Westerhill Road, Bishopbriggs, Glasgow G64 2QT
T: 0141 772 3200; **F**: 0141 306 3119; **W**: www.harpercollins.co.uk
General, fiction, children's, educational, religious, biography, leisure, reference, maps and atlases

HARVEY MAP SERVICES LTD
12–22 Main Street, Doune, Perthshire FK16 6BJ
T: 01786 841202; **E**: sales@harveymaps.co.uk; **W**: www.harveymaps.co.uk
Maps for walking, cycling and rambling

HODDER GIBSON 🅿🅢
2a Christie Street, Paisley PA1 1NB
T: 0141 848 1609; **E**: hoddergibson@hodder.co.uk;
W: www.hoddereducation.co.uk
Educational textbooks and revision guides for the Scottish curriculum

IMPRINT PUBLISHING SYSTEMS LTD
Studio 33, Sir James Clark Building, Seedhill, Paisley PA1 1JT
T: 0141 849 0199; **E**: enquiries@imprintpublishing.co.uk;
W: www.imprintpublishing.co.uk
Education, textbooks and multimedia

JOHN RITCHIE LTD
40 Beansburn,Kilmarnock, East Ayrshire KA3 1RH
T: 01563 536 394; **F**: 01563 571 191; **W**: www.ritchiechristianmedia.co.uk
Christian publisher/distributor

KEA PUBLISHERS
14 Flures Crescent, Erskine, Renfrewshire PA8 7DJ
E: enquiries@keapublishing.com; **W:** www.keapublishing.com
Aviation

KETTILLONIA
Sidlaw House, 24 South Street, Newtyle, Angus PH12 8UQ
T: 01828 650 615; **E:** james@kettillonia.co.uk; **W:** www.kettillonia.co.uk
Poetry and pamphlets, short stories and Kettillonia Journal

KINMORE MUSIC
Shillinghill, Temple, Midlothian EH23 4SH
T: 01875 830 328; **F:** 01875 325 390; **E:** info@templerecords.co.uk;
W: www.templerecords.co.uk
Scottish folk music

KOO PRESS
19 Lochinch Park, Aberdeen AB12 3RF
E: koopoetry@btinternet.com **W:** www.koopress.co.uk
Poetry chapbooks

LEARNING UNLIMITED
Suite 5002, Mile End Mill, 12 Seedhill Road, Paisley PA1 1JS
T: 0141 561 1150; **E:** mail@learningunlimited.co.uk;
W: www.learningunlimited.co.uk
Publications on learning and teaching for teachers

LECKIE & LECKIE LTD PS
4 Queen Street, Edinburgh EH2 1JE
T: 0131 220 6831; **F:** 0131 225 9987; **E:** enquiries@leckieandleckie.co.uk;
W: www.leckieandleckie.co.uk
Scottish teaching, learning and revision

LEXISNEXIS BUTTERWORTHS
London House, 20–22 East London Street, Edinburgh EH7 4BQ
T: 0131 524 1700; **F:** 0131 524 1800; **W:** www.lexisnexis.co.uk
Law

LEXUS LTD
60 Brook Street, Glasgow G40 2AB
T: 0141 556 0440; **F:** 0141 556 2202; **W:** www.lexusforlanguages.co.uk
Foreign language phrasebooks and textbooks

LIBRARIO
Brough House, Milton Brodie, Kinloss, Moray IV36 2UA
T: 01343 850 178; **E:** amlawson@librario.com; **W:** www.librario.com
History, poetry, biographies, travel and fiction

THE LINEN PRESS
75c (13) South Oswald Road, Edinburgh EH9 2HH
E: lynnmichelo@googlemail.com; **W:** www.linenpressbooks.co.uk
Literary fiction and memoirs

LUATH PRESS LTD PS
543/2 Castlehill, The Royal Mile, Edinburgh EH1 2ND
T: 0131 225 4326; **F:** 0131 225 4324; **E:** gavin.macdougall@luath.co.uk;
W: www.luath.co.uk
Fiction and non-fiction including guide books, poetry, social history

MAINSTREAM PUBLISHING PS
7 Albany St, Edinburgh EH1 3UG
T: 0131 557 2959; **F:** 0131 556 8720; **E:** enquiries@mainstreampublishing.com;
W: www.mainstreampublishing.com
General non-fiction, biography, sport and health

MALCOLM CANT PUBLICATIONS
13 Greenbank Row, Edinburgh EH10 5SY
T: 0131 447 6035; **E:** malcolm@edinburghbooks.freeserve.co.uk
Books on Edinburgh's local history

MASTERCLASS MUSIC LTD
12 Kelso Place, Dundee DD2 1SL
T: 01382 667 251; **E:** donmusic@rmplc.co.uk
Instrumental arrangements for secondary schools

MCCALL BARBOUR
28 George IV Bridge, Edinburgh EH1 1ES
T: 0131 225 4816
Bible publisher and Christian books distributor

NATIONAL ARCHIVES OF SCOTLAND **PS**
HM General Register House, Edinburgh EH1 3YY
T: 0131 535 1314; **E:** publications@nas.gov.uk; **W:** www.nas.gov.uk
Scholarly texts, research guides, general historical, educational

NATIONAL GALLERIES OF SCOTLAND PUBLISHING **PS**
Gallery of Modern Art, Belford Road, Edinburgh EH4 3DR
T: 0131 624 6257/6261/6269; **E:** publications@nationalgalleries.org;
W: www.nationalgalleries.org
Art, photography books and catalogues

NATIONAL LIBRARY OF SCOTLAND **PS**
George IV Bridge, Edinburgh EH1 1EW
T: 0131 226 4531; **E:** marketing@nls.uk; **W:** www.nls.uk
Bibliographies, literary and historical

NEIL WILSON PUBLISHING LTD **PS**
G/2 19 Netherton Avenue, Glasgow G13 1BQ
T: 0141 954 8007; **F:** 0560 150 4806; **E:** info@nwp.co.uk; **W:** www.nwp.co.uk
Whisky and beer, hillwalking, sport, Scottish history and humour

THE NEW IONA PRESS **PS**
The Bungalow, Ardival, Strathpeffer, Ross-shire IV14 9DS
T: 01997 421 186; **E:** mairimacarthur@yahoo.co.uk
Local and natural history of Iona and Mull

NGT PUBLISHING LTD
7 Queens Gardens, Aberdeen AB15 4YD
T: 01224 826 337; **E:** info@ngtpublishing.co.uk; **W:** www.ngtpublishing.co.uk
Local history, Burns interest

NICHOLSON MAPS
3 Frazer Street, Largs, Ayrshire KA30 9HP
T: 01475 689 242; **E**: sales@nicholsonmaps.com; **W**: www.nicholsonmaps.com
Maps and street guides

NMS ENTERPRISES LTD – PUBLISHING `PS`
National Museum of Scotland, Chambers Street, Edinburgh EH1 1JF
T: 0131 247 4026; **E**: publishing@nms.ac.uk; **F**: 0131 247 4012; **W**: www.nms.ac.uk
Geology, natural history, Scottish history and culture, educational material and exhibition catalogues

OLIDA PUBLISHING
41 Gaddle Braes, Peterhead AB42 1PJ
Fiction
W: www.olidapublishing.moonfruit.com

OVADA BOOKS
St Mungo's Retreat, 52 Parson St, Glasgow G4 0RX
T/F: 0141 552 5523; **E**: info@ovadabooks.com **W**: www.ovadabooks.com
Religious publications

PERTH AND KINROSS LIBRARIES `PS`
A K Bell Library, York Place, Perth PH2 8EP
T: 01738 444 949; **E**: library@pkc.gov.uk; **W**: www.pkc.gov.uk/library
Local history and general, local authors

POCKET MOUNTAINS LTD
6 Church Wynd, Bo'ness, West Lothian EH51 0AN
T: 01506 500 402; **E**: info@pocketmountains.com;
W: www.pocketmountains.com
Walking guides and active outdoors

THE PUBLISHING CUPBOARD
20 St Vincent Crescent, Glasgow G3 8LQ
T: 0141 248 4780; **W**: www.publishingcupboard.co.uk
Language learning packs

PUMPKIN PRESS
17b St Dennis Terrace, Dundee DD3 9PD
T: 01382 525 904; E: sharon@pumpkinpress.co.uk; W: www.pumpkinpress.co.uk
City guides, Scottish fiction and local interest

RIAS PUBLISHING PS
15 Rutland Square, Edinburgh EH1 2BE
T: 0131 229 7545; E: bookshop@rias.org.uk; W: www.rias.org.uk
Illustrated architectural guides and architectural reference

ROYAL BOTANIC GARDEN EDINBURGH PS
20A Inverleith Row, Edinburgh EH3 5LR
T: 0131 248 2819; E: pps@rbge.org.uk; W: www.rbge.org.uk
Botanical, horticultural interest and scientific

ROYAL COMMISSION ON THE ANCIENT AND HISTORICAL MONUMENTS OF SCOTLAND (RCAHMS) PS
John Sinclair House, 16 Bernard Terrace, Edinburgh EH8 9NX
T: 0131 662 1456; F: 0131 662 1477; E: info@rcahms.gov.uk;
W: www.rcahms.gov.uk
Research, archeological findings and historic maps

RUCKSACK READERS
Landrick Lodge, Dunblane FK15 0HY
T: 01786 824 696; F: 01786 825 090; E: info@rucsacs.com; W: www.rucsacs.com
Walking and guidebooks

SAINT ANDREW PRESS PS
121 George St, Edinburgh EH2 4YN
T: 0131 225 5722 (ext 305); F: 0131 240 2236; E: standrewpress@cofscotland.org.uk;
W: www.churchofscotland.org.uk/standrewpress
Christian and general

THE SALTIRE SOCIETY PS
9 Fountain Close, 22 High Street, Edinburgh EH1 1TF
T: 0131 556 1836; F: 0131 557 1675; E: saltire@saltiresociety.org.uk;
W: www.saltiresociety.org.uk
Scottish/Gaelic history and current affairs

SANDSTONE PRESS `PS`
PO Box 5725, 1 High Street, Dingwall, Ross-shire IV15 9WJ
T/F: 01349 862 583; **E:** info@sandstonepress.com; **W:** www.sandstonepress.com
Non-fiction and adult literacy in both English and Gaelic

SAPIENS PUBLISHING
Duncow, Kirkmahoe, Dumfriesshire DG1 1TA
T: 01387 711 061; **F:** 01387 710 723; **E:** info@sapienspublishing.com;
W: www.sapienspublishing.com
Specialist medical publishers

SARABAND `PS`
Suite 202, 98 Woodlands Road, Glasgow G3 6HB
T: 0141 337 2411; **E:** hermes@saraband.net; **W:** www.saraband.net
Illustrated non-fiction and reference, arts and history

SCOTTISH BIBLE SOCIETY
7 Hampton Terrace, Edinburgh EH12 5XU
T: 0131 337 9701; **F:** 0131 337 0641; **E:** info@scottishbiblesociety.org;
W: www.scottishbiblesociety.org
Christian and religious publications

SCOTTISH BOOK TRUST `PS`
Sandeman House, Trunk's Close, 55 High Street, Edinburgh EH1 1SR
T: 0131 524 0160; **E:** info@scottishbooktrust.com; **W:** www.scottishbooktrust.com
Bibliographies, literary guides and posters

SCOTTISH BRAILLE PRESS
Craigmillar Park, Edinburgh EH16 5NB
T: 0131 662 4445; **F:** 0131 662 1968; **E:** info.sbp@royalblind.org;
W: www.royalblind.org/scottishbraillepress
Alternative formats such as Braille, large print and audio

SCOTTISH CHILDREN'S PRESS AND SCOTTISH CULTURAL PRESS
Unit 6, Newbattle Abbey Business Annexe, Newbattle Road, Dalkeith,
Midlothian EH22 3LJ
T: 0131 660 4757; **F:** 0131 660 6366; **E:** info@scottishbooks.com;
W: www.scottishbooks.com
Books on and from Scotland

SCOTTISH NATURAL HERITAGE PS
Publications Section, Battleby, Redgorton, Perth PH1 3EW
T: 01738 458 530; 01224 654 330; **F:** 01738 827 411; 01224 630 250
E: pam.malcolm@snh.gov.uk; **W:** www.snh.org.uk
General interest, countryside access, environmental and educational

SCOTTISH SOCIETY FOR NORTHERN STUDIES
University of Edinburgh, 27 George Square, Edinburgh EH8 9LD
W: www.northernstudies.org.uk
Scandinavian, Celtic and Scottish culture

SCOTTISH TEXT SOCIETY PS
School of English Studies, University of Nottingham, University Park,
Nottingham NG7 2RD
E: editorialsecretary@scottishtextsociety.org; **W:** www.scottishtextsociety.org
Literary and historical scholarly texts

SERAFINA PRESS PS
The Smokehouse Gallery, St Ellas Place, Eyemouth TD14 5HP
T: 07906 064 982; 01890 752 116; **E:** info@serafinapress.co.uk;
W: www. serafinapress.co.uk
Literary and historical scholarly texts

THE SHETLAND TIMES LTD
Gremista, Lerwick, Shetland ZE1 0PX
T: 01595 693 622; **E:** publishing@shetland-times.co.uk;
W: www.shetland-times.co.uk
Local interest

SHOVING LEOPARD
Flat 2F3, 8 Edina Street, Edinburgh EH7 5PN
T: 0131 477 8197; **E**: info@shovingleopard.com; **W**: www.shovingleopard.com
Spiritual and/or philosophical interest

SPORTSCOTLAND PS
Caledonia House, Redheughs Rigg, South Gyle, Edinburgh EH12 9DQ
T: 0131 472 3207; **E**: library@sportscotland.org.uk; **W**: www.sportscotland.org.uk
Research, promotional, advisory information on sport-related subjects

STENLAKE PUBLISHING
(incorporating Alloway Publishing)
54-58 Mill Square, Catrine, Ayrshire KA5 6RD
T: 01290 551 122; **F**: 01290 551 122; **E**: info@stenlake.co.uk; **W**: www.stenlake.co.uk
Local interest, industry and heritage

STRIDENT PUBLISHING LTD PS
22 Strathwhinnan Drive, Hairmyres, East Kilbride G75 8GT
T: 01355 220 588; **E**: info@stridentpublishing.co.uk;
W: www.stridentpublishing.co.uk
Children's books

TAIGH NA TEUD MUSIC PUBLISHERS
13 Upper Breakish, Isle of Skye IV42 8PYY
T: 01471 822 528; **F**: 01471 822 811; **E**: alasdair@scotlandsmusic.com;
W: www.scotlandsmusic.com
Scottish music and sheet music

TOURIST PUBLICATIONS
5 Eglinton Crescent, Edinburgh EH12 5DH
T: 0131 225 4547; **W**: www.touristpublications.co.uk
Guide maps for Edinburgh and Glasgow

TWO RAVENS PRESS
Green Willow Croft, Rhiroy, Lochbroom, Ullapool, Ross-shire IV23 2SF
T: 01854 655 307; **E**: info@tworavenspress.com; **W**: www.tworavenspress.com
Literary fiction and poetry

VAGABOND VOICES `PS`

3 Sulaisiadar, An Rudha, Isle of Lewis, HS2 0PU
T: 01851 870 050; **E:** sales@vagabondvoices.co.uk; **W:** www.vagabondvoices.co.uk
Literary fiction, non-fiction, poetry and polemics (much of it in translation)

WEST DUNBARTONSHIRE LIBRARIES AND MUSEUMS `PS`

Library HQ, 19 Poplar Road, Dumbarton G82 2RJ
T: 01389 608 045; **F:** 01389 608 044 **E:** ian.baillie@west-dunbartonshire.gov.uk;
W: www.west-dunbarton.gov.uk
Local history

WHITTLES PUBLISHING `PS`

Dunbeath Mains Cottages, Dunbeath, Caithness KW6 6EY
T: 01593 731 333; **E:** info@whittlespublishing.com;
W: www.whittlespublishing.com
Civil engineering, surveying, science, maritime and nautical

WILD GOOSE PUBLICATIONS

4th Floor, Savoy House, 140 Sauchiehall Street, Glasgow G2 3DH
T: 0141 332 6292; **F:** 0141 332 1090; **W:** www.ionabooks.com
Books and CDs reflecting the concerns of the Iona Community

WITHERBY SEAMANSHIP INTERNATIONAL LTD `PS`

4 Dunlop Square, Livingston EH54 8SB
T: 01506 463 227; **E:** info@emailws.com; **W:** www.witherbyseamanship.com
Marine training, reference and regulatory materials

THE XYZ DIGITAL MAP COMPANY

32/9–10, Hardengreen Business Park, Dalhousie Road, Dalkeith EH22 3NX
T: 0131 454 0426; **F:** 0131 454 0443; **W:** www.xyzmaps.com
Digital mapping and aerial photography

Publishing Scotland Network Membership

Features and Benefits of Network Membership

The Publishing Scotland Network was introduced in 2007 to better reflect the widening definition of publishing and provide a new category of membership for all those who offer services to publishers. In the three years since its launch, the Network has expanded and we are now pleased to count among our members editors, designers, literary agents, printers, authors and universities. There are currently 47 members in the network, including our two honorary members Mike Storie and Stephanie Wolfe Murray.

We aim to provide a sense of community for all those working in or with the Scottish publishing industry by acting as a forum where our members can meet and make contacts, learn about changes and opportunities in the creative sector, and as a place they can come to for support and advice.

Network Members are able to take advantage of many benefits. These include a regular programme of members-only events, ranging from seminars on various industry topics to social evenings with great networking opportunities; free entry in the Yearbook; membership rates on Publishing Scotland's training courses; regular bulletins keeping you up to date with news and events from the Scottish book trade, and a 10% discount on all orders from BooksfromScotland.com.

For more information on the Publishing Scotland Network and how to join, please contact Jane Walker (jane@publishingscotland.org) or see our website (www.publishingscotland.org).

List of Network Members

KATE BLACKADDER `NM`

Qualifications and experience: Diploma in Book and Periodical Publishing. Over 25 years' publishing experience in London and Edinburgh.

Services offered: Copy-editing and proofreading general non-fiction, fiction, children's books and corporate literature. Abridging books and short stories.

Clients include: NMS Enterprises – Publishing, Consumer Focus Scotland, Publishing Scotland, Association of Scottish Literary Studies, Deerpark Press, Waverley Books, Whittles Publishing, NGT Publishing, Radio 4, Radio Scotland

Additional information: Membership Secretary of the Edinburgh Writers' Club. Contact details below if you would like an information pack, or visit www.edinburghwritersclub.org.uk

CONTACTS
People: Kate Blackadder
Address: 39 Warrender Park Terrace, Edinburgh EH9 1EB
Tel: 0131 228 4237
Email: kate.blackadder@talk21.com

MARK BLACKADDER NM

Qualifications and experience: Diploma in Art and Design; 19 years as freelance

Equipment: Apple Mac

Services offered: The internal and external design of books

Clients include: ASLS, Birlinn Ltd, Malcolm Cant Publications, Dunedin Academic Press, Fort Publishing, W Green, NMS Enterprises – Publishing, Neil Wilson Publishing and Publishing Scotland

CONTACTS
People: Mark Blackadder
Address: 39 Warrender Park Terrace, Edinburgh EH9 1EB
Tel: 0131 228 4237
Email: m.blackadder@btopenworld.com

BUREAUISM PUBLISHING SERVICES  NM

Qualifications and experience: MA (Hons), Graduate Diploma in Law (Commendation). 8 years' publishing experience in-house and freelance, bringing educational textbooks and e-learning materials from concept through to production. Areas of specialism include EFL, academic publishing, literacy, instructional design for web-based platforms, writing for teachers and young learners, podcasting. Expertise in project management, development editing and content/copy editing.

Clients include: EdExcel, Pearson Longman, EF Education, Garnet Education, Cambridge University Press

Services offered: Editorial project management, content creation (from textbooks to web-based platforms to PowerPoints to Podcasts), in-house training in instructional design and ELT, development editing, copy-editing. Subject specialisms: ELT, Law, Psychology, Religious Studies, Criminology.

CONTACTS
People: Kirsten Campbell
Address: London and Edinburgh
Tel: 07725 951 351
E-mail: kirsten.campbell@bureauism.com
Web: www.bureauism.com

ANDREW BUTTERWORTH NM

Services: Book design, magazine design, page layout, typesetting. Corporate publishing and brand implementation.

CONTACTS
People: Andrew Butterworth
Address: 102/6 Easter Warriston, Edinburgh EH7 4QZ
Tel: 0131 538 6243
Mob: 07984 425 336
Email: arbutterworth@aol.com

JANE CAMILLIN NM

Services: Marketing plans, market research and budget planning. Catalogues, leaflets, direct mail, advanced information sheets, event management and launch events, sponsorship inquiries and applications, UK-wide media relations and publicity campaigns. Experience and advice relating to sales, key accounts, book clubs, export distribution arrangements, websites and new media. Publishing experience includes trade, fiction, reference, academic, schools and children's.

CONTACTS
People: Jane Camillin
Address: 37 St Fillans Crescent, Aberdour, Fife, KY3 0XF
Tel: 07813 093 260
Email: janecamillin@yahoo.co.uk

LUCY CAROLAN **NM**

Copy-editing and proofreading (non-fiction); editing for English as a second language; some specialised areas of translation (French, German and Italian)

CONTACTS
People: Lucy Carolan
Tel: 0131 228 5660
Email: lucy.carolan@tiscali.co.uk

CITY APPOINTMENTS

City Appointments Ltd is an independent recruitment consultancy based in Edinburgh and established in 2004.

We have over 25 years' combined experience in recruitment, including 15 years within the publishing sector. Our specialist consultant, Stuart Pownall, has successfully recruited for editorial, production, design, advertising and subscription sales, business development and general support vacancies for market-leading publishers.

In addition to our expertise in publishing, we also cover a wide range of other disciplines, including: accountancy and finance; charities, NFP and public sector; executive; office support and secretarial and retail and tourism.

We are delighted to offer discounted rates on our permanent, contract and temporary recruitment services to all Publisher and Network Members of Publishing Scotland. If you feel that Stuart's overview of the industry may be beneficial to your organisation, please contact us for an informal discussion on how we can help.

CONTACTS
People: Stuart Pownall
Address: 5a Coates Place, Edinburgh, EH3 7AA
Tel: 0131 623 1010
Fax: 0131 623 1012
Email: s.pownall@cityappointments.com
Website: www.cityappointments.com

CHARLES COVENTRY NM

Qualifications and experience: MA, BPhil, MLitt, Dip TEFL

Services offered: Proofreading and translation into and from Gaelic for the Scottish Government, Mainstream Publishing, Scottish Education Department – now Gaelic proofreader for Scottish Natural Heritage; Cassell Education (Greek), CUP Classics Division (Latin), Floris Books and private clients.

CONTACTS
People: Charles Coventry
Address: 303/3 Colinton Road, Edinburgh EH13 0NR
Tel: 0131 441 7898
Email: charlie.coventry@yahoo.co.uk

☉ CPI GROUP

CPI BOOKS (sponsor member) **NM**

Whatever the run length and wherever the book may be in its life cycle, CPI can provide a cost effective solution. CPI Books can truly offer the service from one to one million copies and it is key to our investment strategy that customer files can be multi-purposed to provide print on demand or high quality ebooks.

So whether the order is for a Man Booker prize winner, regenerating the backlist with POD, ebook conversions and advice, a new business start-up or self publishing, CPI Books have invested to make it cost-effective, quicker and simpler for publishers to get their content to the most important person: the reader.

With a dedicated sales office in Scotland, CPI Books are serious about looking after our existing Scottish customers as well as helping and developing new ones.

CONTACTS
People: Martin McCall
Tel: 01634 671 200
Mobile: 07747 471 582
Email: mmccall@cpi-group.co.uk
Website: www.cpibooks.com

THE CROMWELL PRESS GROUP NM

Services offered: The Cromwell Press Group specialises in the manufacture of books, journals, loose-leaf, cased and limp mono, two and four-colour printing, both litho and digital, and cover/jacket production

Cpod: For all your digital requirements including Print on Demand

Cedric & Chivers: Antiquarian bookbinding and restoration

CONTACTS
People: John Turner
Mobile: 07545 481 834
Address: White Horse Business Park, Aintree Avenue, Trowbridge, Wiltshire BA14 0XB
Tel: 01225 711 400
Fax: 01255 711 429
Email: books@cromwellpressgroup.co.uk
Website: www.cromwellpressgroup.co.uk

Carousel Monkey

GILLIAN DAVIES – PUBLISHING SERVICES **NM**

Qualifications and experience: MA (Hons), LLB. 16 years' publishing experience in-house and freelance, writing, copy-editing, indexing and project management.

I am also a fine artist/illustrator specialising in art for children and the child at heart, with a studio at Gillian Davies, studio 4.35, artscomplex, St Margaret's House, 151 London Road, Edinburgh EH8 7TG 0781 825 3706, Meadowbank.

Art Blog: http://carouselmonkey.blogspot.com

Clients include: A&C Black, Edward Elgar, Lexis Nexis, Smith Bernal, Thomson, Informa.

Specialist areas: law, business, fine art, architecture. My own book on *Copyright for artists, designers and illustrators* will be published by A&C Black in 2010.

Services offered: Project-managing, writing and re-writing, research, editing and proofreading (on-screen and hard copy), permissions, picture research.

CONTACTS
People: Gillian Davies
Address: 2a Fair-A-Far, Cramond EH4 6QD
Tel: 0131 336 4630
Email: lawandarts@aol.com

MORVEN DOONER NM

Services: Project management; general and structural editing of general fiction and non-fiction, reference, education; lexicography; copyediting and proofreading; editing non-native English; copywriting

Experience: 11 years' in-house publishing experience in editorial and management roles at ChambersHarrap, HarperCollins, and Neil Wilson Publishing

CONTACTS
People: Morven Dooner
Tel: 0141 423 9020
Mob: 07799 066 077
Email: morven@mac.com

NICOLAS ECHALLIER NM

Services: Typesetting, design and publishing solutions including book design; typesetting; XML into Indesign; design and layout of marketing materials; project management of external typesetters; web design; IT/technical advice.

CONTACTS
People: Nicolas Echallier
Address: 92/6 East Crosscauseway, Edinburgh EH8 9HQ
Tel: 07912 417 126
Email: nicolas@nicolasechallier.com
Website: www.nicolasechallier.com

EDINBURGH NAPIER UNIVERSITY NM

Proudly celebrating over 40 years as an international centre of excellence in publishing education, Edinburgh Napier University's exciting and intensive postgraduate publishing programmes are designed specifically to prepare you for a career in publishing. As an innovative seat of learning in publishing, Edinburgh Napier is ranked as Scotland's top modern university (Guardian University Guide 2009) and is in the top 10 in the UK for graduate employability (HESA, 2009). We take full advantage of our Edinburgh location, the home of Scottish publishing and the first UNESCO City of Literature, and have developed strong links with the industry, both in Scotland and further afield. Students from all over the world come to study publishing at Napier and graduate with skills in commissioning, editorial, design, marketing, production, e-publishing, management and rights.

Our Postgraduate Publishing programme is located in the Scottish Centre for the Book, a renowned research centre which acts as a focus for research into books and reading (www.napier.ac.uk/scob).

We offer a work placement, which greatly enhances your employment prospects in this highly competitive yet vibrant industry, and students are engaged in live publishing projects, many of which are published via our Merchiston Publishing imprint.

Two postgraduate degrees* will be available for the 2010 intake:
• MSc Publishing
• MSc Magazine Publishing*
* MSc Magazine Publishing is subject to validation

Both degrees offer full-time and part-time study options. PG Cert/PG Dip and MSc awards available.

Edinburgh Napier University also offers customised in-service courses for publishing houses and related organisations, from copy-editing to new production technology.

CONTACTS
People: Avril Gray (Programme Leader, Postgraduate Publishing)
Address: Edinburgh Napier University, School of Arts & Creative Industries, Craighouse Campus, Craighouse Road, Edinburgh EH10 5LG
Tel: 0131 455 6150
Fax: 0131 455 6193
Email: a.gray@napier.ac.uk
Website: www.napier.ac.uk; www.publishingdegree.co.uk

ELLUSTRATION NM

Ellustration is a graphic design agency specialising in the book publishing sector. The company provides the prepress services of illustration, design and page layout, and works extensively with educational, children's and architectural publishers.

In addition to the content and prepress services supplied to our customers, Ellustration also supplies conceptual design for a range of marketing material for our clients and their lists. We also offer graphic design for web-based applications.

Ellustration was set up in 2005 and is based in Edinburgh, but has clients throughout the UK and Spain. Eduardo Iturralde, who is the driving force and creative director of Ellustration, is a native of Madrid and moved to Scotland in 2003. Eduardo graduated from the University of Madrid in Creative Advertising, where he specialised in graphic design. Ellustration makes use of a select group of collaborators, who bring a broad range of skills to the company's portfolio.

CONTACTS
People: Eduardo Iturralde; Dave McCormack
Email: edu@ellustration.net
Website: www.ellustration.net

FOOTEPRINT UK NM

Footeprint UK offers printing, finishing and origination for a complete range of branded business stationery. We can work with you to design logos and artwork, as we have full in-house graphics capabilities. We can also accept ready-to-print graphics in a variety of formats via email or on disc.

We are based in a custom-built packaging factory, which offers state-of-the-art technology with the most current in printing equipment.

We can offer services that help you to reduce your print costs. We produce work in larger runs and where required we can provide storage at no additional cost. We can offer next day delivery as and when you require a call off. Recent clients have included Lloyds TSB, EuroChoices and the Journal of Agriculture Economics.

CONTACTS
People: Fraser Leckie
Address: Riverside Works, Edinburgh Road, Jedburgh, Roxburghshire TD8 6EA
Tel: 01835 862 667
Fax: 01835 862 042
Email: info@footeprint.co.uk
Website: www.footeprint.co.uk

FREIGHT NM

Freight is one of Scotland's leading communications consultancies and has always had a strong involvement in the publishing industry. Freight regularly designs, typesets and publishes books and magazines for a wide range of clients and for its own imprint. Recent book projects include *Revival in Rose Street* for Rutherford House, *Let's Pretend – 37 stories about (in)fidelity* for University of Glasgow and *She Settles in the Shields* for the Glasgow Women's Library.

Periodical projects include alumni magazines for University of Edinburgh and University of West of Scotland, staff magazines for Glasgow City Council and *Gutter*, a magazine of new Scottish writing for the Freight imprint. The company has also worked on a wide range of book jacket design projects for companies such as Black and White, STL, Paternoster and Rutherford House. Publishing projects have also been completed for Chambers, National Galleries of Scotland and Scottish Refugee Council.

Freight is based in Glasgow and works with a wide range of commercial, public and third sector organisations across brand identity, literature, web, exhibitions and packaging. The company regularly wins creative awards for its work.

CONTACTS
People: Adrian Searle, Laura Henderson
Address: 49-53 Virginia Street, Glasgow, G1 1TS
Tel: 0141 552 5303
Email: info@freightdesign.co.uk
Website: www.freightdesign.co.uk

GILLIAN CLOKE PUBLISHING SERVICES NM

Qualifications and experience: MA (Hons), MPhil, History. 10 years' publishing experience in-house and freelance, in all areas of commissioning, project management, development and editing. Also a published author in my own right (Routledge), so experience of both sides of the divide!

Professional appointments include: Publishing Consultant for the Royal Commission on Ancient and Historical Monuments of Scotland (RCAHMS), Equalities and Human Rights Commission (EHRC), Development Editor for Elsevier Health Sciences, Publications Manager for the Church of Scotland's Board of Parish Education. Freelance clients include Rutland Press (now RIAS Publishing), RCAHMS, Elsevier, National Christian Educational Council, Scottish Christian Press, BookChase.

Services offered: Complete range of publishing services – trouble-shooting a speciality! Project-managing, writing and rewriting, research, editing and proofreading (on-screen and hard copy), reference-checking, permissions, consultancy. Will take on most subjects but particularly experienced in education, history, humanities, literature and religious; experienced also in medical, musical and architecture; competent in classical languages and experienced in medical, classical and ecclesiastical Latin.

CONTACTS
People: Gillian Cloke
Address: 16 Buckstone Close, Edinburgh EH10 6XA
Tel: 0131 622 0644
Email: gill.cloke@virgin.net

GRAVEMAKER+SCOTT NM

Gravemaker+Scott have a wide and varied international experience in the design, typesetting and production of books, catalogues, magazines and printed matter.

We regularly write articles on design, interiors and architecture for several magazines in the UK and abroad.

Thomas Gravemaker was born and trained in Amsterdam, he moved to London in the early 1980s, where he worked with several book publishers. At the end of the 1980s he moved to Paris, where he set up his own studio, working for museums and publishers in France. Another move, to Edinburgh, followed in 2007, where he established Gravemaker+Scott with Christine Scott.

Scottish born Christine Scott trained in Newcastle-upon-Tyne. She has worked in fashion, design and forecasting in London, Paris and Amsterdam, before moving into design consultancy, working as a consultant with Aveda and Bumble & Bumble.

Clients include: Ammonite Press, Blueprint, Flammarion, Frame Magazine, L'Institut de France, The Louvre, National Galleries of Scotland, Centre Georges Pompidou, Print, La Réunion des Musées Nationaux, Éditions du Regard, Musée Rodin, Sandstone Press, Scottish Poetry Library and Thames & Hudson.

CONTACTS
People: Thomas Gravemaker and Christine Scott
Address: 7 Almond Bank Cottages, Whitehouse Road, Edinburgh EH4 6PJ
Tel: 0131 336 1383
Paris address: 17-19, rue beautreiilis, 75004 Paris
Tel: + 33 (0)1 48 04 53 80
Email: tomscot@btinternet.com

JENNY BROWN ASSOCIATES NM

Founded in 2002, Jenny Brown Associates has quickly become one of the leading literary agencies in the UK, the biggest literary agent in Scotland and a literary agent with a worldwide reputation. Jenny Brown and Mark Stanton represent over 80 writers of fiction (both literary and commercial) and non-fiction (sport, history and biography), while Allan Guthrie and Lucy Juckes specialise in crime fiction and children's books respectively. Clients include Lin Anderson, Alasdair Gray, Alex Gray, Keith Gray, Stona Fitch, Sara Maitland, Richard Moore, Natasha Solomon, Kenneth Steven, and Paul Torday.

Many of the agency's clients are based in Scotland, which allows a close working relationship between writer and agent, but the company sells work to publishers worldwide. Jenny Brown Associates is a member of The Association of Authors' Agents and The Association of Scottish Literary Agents. Please see website for submission details.

CONTACTS

People: Jenny Brown, Mark Stanton, Allan Guthrie, Lucy Juckes, Kevin Pocklington (Foreign Rights)

Address: 33 Argyle Place, Edinburgh EH9 1JT

Tel: 0131 229 5334

Email: info@jennybrownassociates.com

Website: www.jennybrownassociates.com

THE JUDY MOIR AGENCY NM

The Judy Moir Agency was established in June 2008 and specialises in adult fiction and non-fiction of many kinds, with a particular emphasis on Scottish writing. Judy has worked for many publishers in Scotland over the last 25 years or so, including Mainstream Publishing, Canongate Books and Penguin Scotland, as well as doing occasional freelance editing for a wide range of UK publishers. She was a former director of the Scottish Publishers Association in the early 1980s and for a while also lectured on the publishing course at Edinburgh Napier University. Currently she also serves as a Special Advisor to the Literature Department of the Scottish Arts Council.

Submissions: Authors are very welcome to make contact, either by email or by letter – in the first instance, please do not send manuscripts, just a few paragraphs on your writing.

CONTACTS
People: Judy Moir
Address: 5 Gayfield Square, Edinburgh EH1 3NW
Tel: 0131 557 1771
Email: judy_moir@blueyonder.co.uk

THE MCKERNAN LITERARY AGENCY AND CONSULTANCY **NM**

Small literary agency and consultancy providing a very personal and meticulous service to writers of all kinds. Founded 2005. Maggie McKernan handles literary and commercial fiction and non-fiction: Scottish, biography, history, current affairs, memoirs; Edwin Hawkes handles fiction (especially science fiction, fantasy and historical fiction) and non-fiction (popular history, politics and science). We sell to the UK market, and work with the London agency Capel & Land for translation, US, film and TV sales. No reading fee.

Authors include Michael Collins, Alan Taylor, Belinda Seaward, Michael Fry, Michael Schmidt and Carlos Alba.

For submission details and for further information on services offered, please see www.mckernanagency.co.uk.

CONTACTS
People: Maggie McKernan and Edwin Hawkes
Address: 5 Gayfield Square, Edinburgh EH1 3NW
Tel: 0131 557 1771
Email: maggie@mckernanagency.co.uk AND edwin@mckernanagency.co.uk
Website: www.mckernanagency.co.uk

HELEN D MCPHERSON NM

I offer a range of publishing and editorial services, including project management, editing, copy-editing, proofreading, commissioning, list development and management, journal development and management, research, and competitor analysis. I am happy to work on-screen or from hard copy, and can work using MS Office or LaTeX.

I specialise in physical sciences and engineering, but I am willing to undertake projects in any non-fiction subject area.

I have over 25 years' experience in publishing, including 10 years editing, commissioning and project managing multi-volume reference works at Pergamon/Elsevier, four years as Senior Publishing Editor for chemistry and chemical engineering at Elsevier, and five years as Publisher for chemistry and materials science at Wiley.

I turned freelance in 2002. Clients include Wiley, Oxford University Press, Nelson Thornes, Scottish Qualifications Authority, Learning and Teaching Scotland, Whittles Publishing, CRC Press, ISTE and Edanz.

CONTACTS
People: Dr Helen D McPherson
Address: 32 Restalrig Road, Edinburgh EH6 8BN
Tel: 0131 553 5451
Fax. 0131 553 5451
Email: hdmcpherson@btinternet.com

SHARON MCTEIR, CREATIVE PUBLISHING SERVICES NM

Qualifications and experience: BA Publishing, 1992. 17 years' publishing experience in-house and freelance. I was design and prepress manager at Chambers Harrap Publishers until 2005 when I went freelance offering design, typesetting and picture research services.

Clients include: Hodder Education, Chambers Harrap, Canongate, Birlinn, Larousse

Services offered

Design and Typesetting: dictionaries and reference material designed and typeset in Arbortext 3B2. Text and image integrated books (internal and external) worked on in Indesign or Quark Xpress. I am also experienced in designing and producing promotional material, catalogues and stationery.

Picture Research: I source either from list supplied by client or directly from manuscript, and work with image libraries to get quotes and to clear copyright. I have experience of working with museums, galleries and private individuals to get suitable images. I also commission illustrators and photographers.

CONTACTS
People: Sharon McTeir
Address: Lavender Cottage, Oldhamstocks, Dunbar TD13 5XN
Tel: 01368 830 338
Email: sharon.mcteir@zen.co.uk

MARY O'NEILL NM

Qualifications and experience: MA (Hons) English Language and Literature (first class). 17 years' in-house publishing experience at Chambers Harrap and HarperCollins, which included list development, commissioning, project management, research, lexicography, content creation, editing and proofreading.

Services offered: Editorial project management; lexicography; copy-editing and proofreading, on screen and on hard copy. Particular experience in dictionaries, general reference, and educational publications and materials.

CONTACTS
People: Mary O'Neill
Address: 3/1, 70 Torrisdale Street, Glasgow G42 8PJ
Tel: 0141 423 5019
Mob: 07765 838 095
Email: mary.oneill@gmail.com

ORCHID

Need a helping hand to move out of the gloom and doom? Want to focus on the success of your organisation?

Whether you are a multi-national company, small business or self-employed, Orchid has an excellent track record of success in providing Personal Focus Programmes for people in business, the public sector, education and the Arts, including writers and musicians.

Orchid provides:
• Personal Focus Programmes to help staff build confidence, lower stress and focus for success
• Move Forward with Confidence Programmes for young people
• Tutor training
• Talks
• New Life Self-Esteem public courses
• Books
• CDs

Patricia Cleghorn, Principal of Orchid, has an exceptionally wide range of experience in helping people to flourish and is author of *The Secrets of Self-Esteem, 30 Minutes to Boost Your Self-Esteem*, and a series of CDs.

The CD *Learn to Relax & Sleep Well!* is faring well in GP trials – confirms our feedback.

Our *Move Forward with Confidence* Tutor Training programme is up and running, allowing many more young people to benefit.

More organisations are benefiting from our new shorter sessions – effective and affordable.

To discuss how we can help you, please get in contact.

CONTACTS
People: Patricia Cleghorn, Principal
Address: 16 Tyrie Avenue, Kirkcaldy KY1 1GB
Tel: 01592 201 333
Email: orchid2100@aol.com
Website: www.orchidinternational.co.uk

OSBORN EDITORIAL SERVICES NM

Lawrence Osborn is an experienced freelance copy-editor and proofreader who works both with hard copy and on-screen in a variety of media including books, CD-ROMs, encyclopaedias, journals and online materials. He has a strong academic background spanning the physical sciences and theology. In addition to working on general fiction and non-fiction, he specialises in astronomy, physics, cultural studies, religious studies, theology and philosophy.

Recent clients include Berg Publishers, Birlinn Ltd, Lion Hudson, Oxford University Press, SCM-Canterbury Press, Solaris Press and TFInforma.

CONTACTS
People: Dr Lawrence Osborn
Address: Flat 35, 250 Camphill Avenue, Glasgow G41 3AS
Tel: 0141 636 1614
Email: editor@lhosborn.co.uk

PAT BAXTER LANGUAGE SERVICES NM

Around ten years' experience as copy-editor/proofreader. Training through SfEP includes on-screen editing courses, and proofreading for the web. Prior career experience in accounting and audit. Editing clients mainly public sector and academic publishers, but also specialising in theses/dissertations from non-English speakers.

Clients include: Local authority and central government organisations; universities of London (Institute of Education), Dundee, West of Scotland; masteral and doctoral postgraduate students from Dundee, Edinburgh, Glasgow and West of Scotland universities; academic authors include SAGE, Taylor & Francis, Routledge, Macmillan, McGraw-Hill.

Services offered: Copy-editing (hard copy and on-screen including websites), proofreading, re-writing, transcription. Specialist subject areas include education, accounting, languages (French, Latin), classical studies, history of art, English language/literature, general subjects, ESOL/TEFL.

CONTACTS
People: Pat Baxter
Address: 104 Demondale Road, Arbroath DD11 1TW
Tel/Fax: 01241 875 040
Mobile: 07799 761 512
Email: patbaxter@btinternet.com

PREPRESS PROJECTS NM

Company overview: We produce books, reports, journals and magazines for academic publishers and public sector organisations. We focus on the humanities, science and medicine and have extensive experience of managing projects from raw copy to final publication. With 18 resourceful staff we are able to put together a knowledgeable team to meet the needs of unusual projects.

Clients include: Health Scotland, Horizon Press, National Health Service, Scottish Natural Heritage, Taylor & Francis, Welsh Assembly Government, Wiley-Blackwell

Services offered: We provide a full publishing project management service including editorial office management, copy-editing, design, typesetting, illustration, proofreading, indexing and XML creation. For some clients we also provide science/technology journalism, picture research and print and distribution management services.

CONTACTS
People: Helen MacDonald (Managing Director)
Address: Prepress Projects Ltd, Algo Business Centre, Glenearn Road, Perth PH2 0NJ
Tel: 01738 450 490
Fax: 0870 164 0124
Email: helen.macdonald@prepress-projects.co.uk
Website: www.prepress-projects.co.uk

PROJECT ONE PUBLISHING SOLUTIONS

Project One Publishing Solutions is an editorial and publishing consultancy run by two experienced educational and academic publishers: Fiona McDonald and Tony Wayte. We have over 35 years' experience as editors and publishers in the UK and Australia, having worked in-house for market-leading publishers such as OUP, Chapman and Hall, Blackwell and Reed Education. This professional expertise is supported by strong backgrounds in the humanities and sciences. Recent clients have included: Bright Red Publishing, Pearson Education, Hodder International and Edexcel. In addition to our work in educational publishing we have also worked on a TV tie-in with BBC Scotland's 'The Adventure Show' for Mountain Media's first book, *The Sutherland Trail*.

As an editorial and publishing consultancy, we can offer a full range of services to help publishers, including:
- Full project management (from initial concept to printer-ready files)
- List development
- Commissioning of projects
- Author briefing
- Manuscript development
- Writing and ghost-writing
- Managing and co-ordinating multi-component (print and electronic) projects and highly-illustrated series
- Freelance design contacts
- Editing and proofreading
- Market research and competition analysis

If you have too much to do, and not enough time or people to do it all, we can help!

CONTACTS
People: Fiona McDonald and Tony Wayte
Address: 20 Dollerie Terrace, Crieff PH7 3EG
Tel: 01764 655 654
Email: info@projectonepublishing.co.uk
Website: www.projectonepublishing.co.uk

REDHOUSE LANE COMMUNICATIONS NM

Qualifications and experience: Redhouse Lane is an award-winning integrated communications agency enabling public and private sector clients to engage their internal and external audiences, creating powerful brand propositions and compelling ways to express and implement them.

Clients include: RBS, NatWest, Scottish & Newcastle, The Glenmorangie, Capability Scotland, Russell Europe, Department of Health, Peugeot Citroën, Business Stream, Active Stirling, BAA, Forestry Commission Scotland, Tesco Bank, Intec plc.

Services offered: With over 70 employees across two locations, including more than 50 project staff – digital and print designers, copywriters and content editors, back and front end developers, project managers, consultants and account managers – we provide a complete end to end solution for our clients' marketing and communications strategies.

Our service offer covers brand origination and development, corporate publishing, design and marketing, content and editorial, internal communications consultancy, digital media strategy and design.

Recent Awards: CiB, CiB Scotland, PPA Scotland, Marketing Effectiveness Awards, FEIEA

CONTACTS
People: Steve Mills (Managing Director)
Address: 4th Floor, The Hatrack, 144 St Vincent Street, Glasgow G2 5LQ
Tel: 0141 225 0890
Fax: 0141 225 0891
Email: stephenm@redhouselane.com
Website: www.redhouselane.com

ABI SAFFREY EDITORIAL SERVICES NM

Qualifications and experience: BA (Hons) Languages and Linguistics. Eight years' in-house editorial experience with business-to-business publishers, trade publishers and non-departmental public bodies. Freelance copy-editor and proofreader since January 2009. Society for Editors and Proofreaders Ordinary member.

Clients include: Cengage Learning, Edward Elgar Publishing, Hodder Education, Learning and Teaching Scotland, Oxford University Press

Services offered: Copy-editing and proofreading (on-screen and hard copy). I have a wide variety of experience in education (policy, guidance, teacher and student support materials), economics, ELT/EFL and politics, but will happily take on work in other social/humanities subject areas.

CONTACTS
People: Abi Saffrey
Address: 11 Crown Gardens, Glasgow G12 9HL
Tel: 0141 334 0803
Email: edit@abisaffrey.co.uk
Website: www.abisaffrey.co.uk

SCA PACKAGING PRINT & SUPPLY CHAIN SOLUTIONS NM

SCA Packaging Print & Supply Chain Solutions provides a full prepress, printing, finishing and warehouse/distribution service to its clients in several market sectors.

SCA Packaging P&SCS offers the latest in prepress solutions including secure FTP connection and server security ensuring your files are in safe hands. Our digital workflow combined with our highly trained prepress technicians will handle all your file management and version control needs. From file receipt to printed product you can be assured that your data integrity and any colour management wishes will be controlled using the latest technology.

Single colour printing is produced on our two web presses with 2 and 4 colour printing on Heidelberg B1 presses. Our finishing processes include wire stitching, perfect binding, folding, drilling and shrink wrapping. We also offer mono and colour digital printing for low volumes on Xerox presses.

In addition to the printed products on offer we can supply CDs/DVDs with product fulfilment, storage and distribution services.

The IT function of the business supports the development of supply chain models to suit customer requirements using e-commerce tools such as EDI and the internet.

Enterprise Resource Planning (ERP) software is utilised throughout the business functions such as procurement, customer services, planning and our warehouse to control purchase order and sales order processing, bill of materials, material requirement planning (MRP) and stock control.

SCA Packaging P&SCS adheres to ISO 9001 and PS 9000:2001 (Pharmaceutical) Quality Assurance standards and the OHSAS 18001 Health & Safety standard.

CONTACTS
People: Alan McKinlay
Address: 166 Riverford Road, Pollokshaws, Glasgow G43 1PT
Tel: 0141 632 0999
Fax: 0141 632 8111
Email: alan.mckinlay@sca.com
Website: www.sca.com

SCOTPRINT (sponsor member) **NM**

Scotprint's exceptional book production facilities provide a quick route to market for a wide range of cased, sewn-limp, slotted/perfect bound, PUR and wire-stitched books.

Our press facilities include three large-format 7B presses and two B1 10-colour perfecting presses. These latest generation presses include colour management and reel-to-sheet technology, which ensures rapid turnaround and excellent colour quality and consistency.

Scotprint is accredited to ISO 14001:2004 (Environmental Management System) and is a custodian of FSC & PEFC. Our company has formal plans to continue development of its excellent environmental profile.

CONTACTS
People: Norrie Gray
Address: Gateside Commerce Park, Haddington, East Lothian EH14 3ST
Tel: 01620 828 800
Fax: 01620 828 801
Mobile: 07966 531 105
Email: info@scotprint.co.uk
Website: www.scotprint.co.uk

SCOTTISH LANGUAGE DICTIONARIES NM

Scottish Language Dictionaries (SLD) are the stewards of the *Scottish National Dictionary* and *A Dictionary of the Older Scottish Tongue*. These monumental dictionaries, along with the 2005 supplement to the *Scottish National Dictionary* are available free, as the *Dictionary of the Scots Language*, at www.dsl.ac.uk.

Smaller works, published by Edinburgh University Press, such as the scholarly single volume *Concise Scots Dictionary*, the *Scots Thesaurus* and the *Essential Scots Dictionary*, recommended for use in schools, are based on these authoritative works.

SLD are currently working on a new edition of the *Concise Scots Dictionary*, a project which will take five years. The small books in the *Say it in Scots* series, published by Black & White Publishing, are ideal as souvenirs and gifts.

Research work at SLD aims to provide an increasingly accurate and comprehensive record of the Scots language from its beginnings to the present day. We also provide outreach services, promoting Scots and bringing the work of the dictionaries to schools and community groups.

CONTACTS
People: Chris Robinson
Address: 25 Buccleuch Place, Edinburgh EH8 9LN
Tel: 0131 650 4149
Fax: 0131 650 4149
Email: mail@scotsdictionaries.org.uk
Website: www.scotsdictionaries.org.uk; www.scuilwab.org.uk; www.dsl.ac.uk

THE SOCIETY OF AUTHORS IN SCOTLAND NM

The Society of Authors is an independent trade union, representing published writers' interests in all aspects of the writing profession, including book and periodical publishing, new media, broadcasting, television and films and has over 550 members in Scotland. The Society of Authors has specialist groups for broadcasters, children's writers, translators, medical, scientific and technical writers and illustrators. It also provides expert contractual advice to members.

The Society of Authors in Scotland campaigns on literary issues in Scotland, organises many and varied events for members and guests throughout Scotland and provides a very popular strand of practical talks and workshops, 'The Writing Business', at the Edinburgh International Book Festival.

CONTACTS
People: Caroline Dunford (Honorary Secretary)
Address: 17 Pittville St Lane, Edinburgh EH15 2BU
Tel: 0131 657 1391
Email: verdandiweaves@mac.com

The Society of Authors Headquarters
Address: 84 Drayton Gardens, London SW10 9SB
Tel: 020 7373 6642
Fax: 020 7373 5768
Website: www.societyofauthors.net

ANNA STEVENSON NM

Qualifications and experience: MA Hons (French and German), 15 years' in-house and freelance experience. Publishing Manager with Chambers Harrap Publishers until 2009, specializing in bilingual dictionaries and language learning.

Services: Complete range of publishing and editing services: project management from initial concept through to finished product; general editing across a broad range of genres including reference, trade and academic; translation (French-English); lexicography; copy-editing; proofreading; author liaison; copywriting; rewriting; non-native English.

Clients include: EUP, Mainstream Publishing.

CONTACTS
People: Anna Stevenson
Tel: 07747 127 296
Email: annastevenson@hotmail.com

UNIVERSITY OF STIRLING – CENTRE FOR INTERNATIONAL PUBLISHING AND COMMUNICATION NM

We teach two postgraduate degree courses at Stirling: the MLitt in Publishing Studies and the MSc in International Publishing Management. Both are regularly fully-subscribed, with course members joining us from all over the world. It is also possible to undertake research leading to a PhD, and staff from the Centre are involved in research and consultancy with a number of partner institutions.

We equip our students with the qualities and skills they will need for a successful working life in publishing, whether working for a large corporation, a small company or any organisation that has a publishing dimension. Increasingly, we focus on electronic delivery and the implications of publishing in the digital age.

Our graduates occupy senior positions in publishing in many countries; we listen to their ideas and experience as we change and modify the course. They tell us that the time and money they have invested in the course has provided them with a continuing advantage in their working lives.

If you would like to come and talk to us about either of our degree courses, or about research opportunities, please do get in touch with us.

CONTACTS
People: Professor Claire Squires
Address: Stirling Centre for International Publishing and Communication, Department of English Studies, Pathfoot Building, University of Stirling, Stirling FK9 4LA
Tel: 01786 467 505
Fax: 01786 466 210
Email: claire.squires@stir.ac.uk
Website: www.publishing.stir.ac.uk

THOMSON LITHO LTD (sponsor member) **NM**

Thomson Litho is Scotland's largest independently-owned printer. We are FSC/ PEFC accredited and have been servicing the publishing industry and various other market sectors for more than 40 years.

From our award-winning 300,000 square foot facility, we offer mono and two-colour litho printing on our B1 Variquik webs; 2, 5 and 6 colour litho printing on our B1 Heidelberg sheet-fed presses; and monochrome digital printing on our Xerox printers. Our Muller Martini Bolero 21-station binding line has the capability of binding 8,000 books per hour.

Our state-of-the-art prepress system runs on a Heidelberg print ready system calibrated to our presses and we can offer data-merging capabilities.

We have a comprehensive suite of finishing facilities including perfect binding, PUR, sewn, notch, double-wire stitching, loose leaf, drilling, folding, lamination, and shrink wrapping. We also offer in-house CD-ROM, DVD, CD-R, DVD-R manufacturing; secure end-user fulfilment and mailing services which can be tailored to your needs. Please see display advert on p 167.

CONTACTS
People: Yvonne Cochrane, Sales Manager
Address: 10 Colvilles Place, Kelvin Industrial Estate, East Kilbride, Glasgow G75 0SN
Tel: 01355 233 081
Fax: 01355 572 083
Mob: 07733 009 552
Email: ycochrane@tlitho.co.uk
Website: www.thomsonlitho.com

TOTAL PUBLISHING SOLUTIONS NM

Hello! My name is Sue Moody. I specialise in research, writing, rewriting and editing and have undertaken many different types of brief since I set up Total Publishing Solutions in 2004.

I mainly work for the education sector, since that's what I know about (I used to be head of publishing at Learning and Teaching Scotland). Clients range from local education authorities and SQA to Scottish Opera and the National Library of Scotland.

I research and write learning and teaching packs, teacher and pupil guides, evaluation studies, research studies and case studies.

I also do rewriting and editing for a variety of clients, including SQA and Learning Unlimited.

I am a member of the Society for Editors and Proofreaders.

CONTACTS
People: Sue Moody (Director)
Address: Total Publishing Solutions Ltd, Wellbrae House, Wellbrae, Falkland KY15 7AY
Tel: 01337 857 097
Mob: 07855 955 517
Email: susan.moody@btinternet.com

TRIWORDS NM

Triwords specialises in on-screen and developmental editing, editing non-native English, research and editorial management, particularly in the fields of medical education, social sciences, policy and management.

Triwords also provides website testing and management of content, proofreading and writing services, fact-checking and liaison with authors.

Types of media handled by Triwords include distance-learning materials, examination papers, online materials, student and faculty handbooks, theses, newsletters, annual reports and business plans, publicity materials, academic journals and book chapters.

Clients include: an international non-profit-making medical organisation based in mainland Europe; Radboud University Nijmegen, the Netherlands; and local SMEs.

Triwords is based in North East Fife and run by Kathleen Brown. Kathleen is a member of the Society for Editors and Proofreaders and Immediate Past Chair of Women Ahead in Dundee and Angus (a business networking organisation). Kathleen worked in local government in Scotland before heading to the USA in 1996. For two years, she was the Publications Editor and Writing Consultant for a medical college in Philadelphia. On her return to Scotland, she worked for the University of Dundee before turning freelance in 2000. Triwords Ltd was established in 2003.

CONTACTS
People: Kathleen Brown (Director)
Address: 12 Sandyhill Road, Tayport, Fife
DD6 9NX
Tel: 01382 553 172
Fax: 01382 553 172 (by arrangement)
Mobile: 07990 646 864
Skype: triwords
Email: kbrown@triwords.co.uk
Website: www.triwords.co.uk

THE TYPEHOUSE (ALISTAIR WARWICK) NM

Qualifications and experience: BMus(Hons), MMus, CertTh. 18 years high-quality music and text typesetting; 11 years proofreading; 8 years web design and development. Also a professional musician (organist and conductor) and published arranger/composer (The Art of Music, Geoffrey Chapman, RSCM).

Clients include: Ashgate, Church House Publishing, Panel of Monastic Musicians, Plainsong & Medieval Music Society, The Royal School of Church Music, SCM-Canterbury Press, University of Wales Press.

Services offered: Typesetting (InDesign), music setting/engraving (SCORE), web design and development (experienced in XHTML/CSS/PHP), proofreading (on-screen and hard copy). Will take on most subjects but particularly experienced in music, history, humanities and religious; experienced in ecclesiastical Latin.

CONTACTS
People: Alistair Warwick
Address: 25 Ramsay Drive, Dunblane FK15 0NG
Tel: 01786 823 000
Mobile: 07792 566 349
Email: info@thetypehouse.co.uk
Website: www.thetypehouse.co.uk

GALE WINSKILL, WINSKILL EDITORIAL NM

I have been an editor for more than fifteen years, in Hong Kong and the UK, and hold Advanced Membership of the Society for Editors and Proofreaders.

I offer a range of services, including: copy-editing and proofreading (on hard copy or on-screen); workshops; literary critiques; rewriting; editing material by non-native speakers of English; Anglicizing or Americanizing; project management and list development. I am fluent in Italian and have a good working knowledge of French and German.

I specialize in children's fiction. Some of my authors have won and/or been shortlisted for the Royal Mail Book Awards (2007–2009 inclusive) and The Kelpies Prize, and longlisted for The Branford Boase Award (2009).

I returned to freelancing in 2008 and now work regularly on children's and adult fiction, adult non-fiction, academic theses and journal articles, and picture books. I also give workshops on various aspects of editing, publishing and freelancing.

My clients include publishing companies, businesses, organizations, academics, literary and translation agencies and private individuals.

CONTACTS
People: Gale Winskill
Address: 90 Main Street, Aberdour, KY3 0UH
Tel: 01383 860 001
Mobile: 0790 523 9781
Email: gale@winskilleditorial.co.uk
Website: www.winskilleditorial.co.uk

WORDSENSE EDITING AND TYPESETTING SERVICES NM

Qualifications and experience: City & Guilds Licentiateship Award in Editorial Skills, Advanced member of the Society for Editors and Proofreaders (SfEP), NVQ Book Editing Level 3 Units 1, 2 & 4, SfEP registered proofreader, SfEP registered copy-editor. I am an editor, proofreader and typesetter who provides a reliable, efficient and friendly service. I have been in business since 1981. I am equally comfortable handling any or all editorial, design and typesetting tasks involved in producing an illustrated or unillustrated book, magazine or brochure, from delivery by an author through to PDFs.

Recent clients: Dorling Kindersley, Mitchell Beazley, Dunedin Academic Press, Frontline Books, Conran Octopus, Equality & Human Rights Commission, Hamlyn, HarperCollins, Faber and Faber, Exeter Civic Society

Services offered: Copy-editing on screen and hard copy; rewriting; typesetting; project management; proofreading; consultancy (editorial); desk-top publishing; liaison with author, and collation of author corrections; page layout; research; and web page/site content checking. I have edited material on a wide range of subjects but my main expertise is in gardening/horticulture and sports (general, cricket, golf, soccer, tennis, walking, winter).

CONTACTS
People: Joanna Chisholm
Address: 11 Dryden Place, Edinburgh EH9 1RP
Tel: 0131 667 5909
Email: joanna@wordsense.co.uk
Website: www.wordsense.co.uk

ZEBEDEE DESIGN & TYPESETTING SERVICES NM

Zebedee Design & Typesetting Services specialises in book design, typesetting, marketing materials and publishing. With extensive experience of working with major publishers, Zebedee Design has worked on titles as varied as dictionaries to sports books, and multi-language to children's books.

Zebedee Design are passionate about providing clients with a bespoke service meeting their specific needs, whilst also providing guidance and additional ideas along the way. Close collaboration is the key to powerful and visually outstanding layout and design.

Becky Pickard has over 10 years experience of working in the publishing field and this broad experience of running various production and design departments has equipped her to view each project with a fresh perspective, and clear vision of what the finished product might look like, and what needs to be done to achieve this.

The services that are provided cover the whole design process, however, if your requirement is a bespoke service in a particular area we would be delighted to advise and assist.

Services: Internal layout and design of books up to printer-ready final pdfs; design and layout of covers and jackets from detailed brief or original concept; catalogue and brochure layout; xml into Indesign; styling and formatting of Word documents; keying; hi-res scanning; picture research.

CONTACTS
People: Becky Pickard
Address: Zebedee Design & Typesetting Services, 4 Markle Steading,
Nr East Linton, East Lothian, EH40 3EB
Tel: 07989 113 559
Email: bek@zebedeedesign.co.uk
Website: www.zebedeedesign.co.uk

Services

ScottishBallet: Forty years

FOOTBALL'S COMIC BOOK HEROES
ADAM RICHES with TIM PARKER and ROBERT FRANKLAND

ALBERTO MORROCCO 1917-1998

Tales from African Dreamtime
YOUNG and KELLER

ESOL for Scottish Qualifications Student's Book
Magdalene Sacranie

DISCOVERING SCOTLAND'S LOST RAILWAYS
David Maule

Chambers
The Chambers Dictionary

Wanderings with a Camera in Scotland
RCAHMS

THE GLASGOW COOKERY BOOK

a life of osprey
rou dennis
IN COMMAND

Easter the Showjumper
H. M

Introduction

The businesses and individuals listed in the following pages provide services to publishers in Scotland at all stages of the publishing process, from proofreading to printing. Along with their contact details, their particular areas of expertise are listed to help you find the right person for your job.

Entries marked **NM** are members of the Publishing Scotland Network – see their detailed profiles on pp 102–146 or on the Publishing Scotland website: www. publishingscotland.org. For more information on how to become a member, please see p 101.

GILLIAN DAVIES NM
studio 4.35, artscomplex, St Margaret's House, 151 London Road, Edinburgh EH8 7TG
T/F: 0131 336 4630; **M**: 07818 253 706
E: lawandarts@aol.com
Services: Art and design, collage, illustration, jewellery. *See also* EDITORIAL SERVICES

Design Services

MARK BLACKADDER NM
39 Warrender Park Terrace, Edinburgh EH5 1EB
T: 0131 228 4237
E: m.blackadder@btopenworld.com
Services: The internal and external design of books

ANDREW BUTTERWORTH NM
102/6 Easter Warriston, Edinburgh EH7 4QZ
T: 0131 538 6243; **M**: 07984 425 336
E: arbutterworth@aol.com
Services: Book design, magazine design, page layout, typesetting.
Corporate publishing and brand implementation.

NICOLAS ECHALLIER NM
Typesetting, Design and Publishing Solutions
92/6 East Crosscauseway, Edinburgh EH8 9HQ
T: 07912 417 126
E: nicolas@nicolasechallier.com; **W**: www.nicolasechallier.com
Services: Book design; typesetting; XML into Indesign; design and layout
of marketing materials; project management of external typesetters;
web design; IT/technical advice

FREIGHT NM
49-53 Virginia Street, Glasgow G1 1TS
T: 0141 552 5303
E: info@freightdesign.co.uk; **W**: www.freightdesign.co.uk
Services: Design, typesetting and production of books, catalogues, magazines
and other printed matter, brand identity, web, exhibitions, packaging

GRAVEMAKER+SCOTT NM
7 Almond Bank Cottages, Whitehouse Road, Edinburgh EH4 6PJ
T: 0131 336 1383
17-19, rue Beautreillis, 75004 Paris
T: + 33 (0)1 48 04 53 80
E: tomscot@btinternet.com
Services: Design, typesetting and production of books, catalogues, magazines
and other printed matter

SHARON McTEIR NM
Lavender Cottage, Oldhamstocks, Dunbar TD13 5XN
T: 01368 830 338
E: sharon.mcteir@zen.co.uk
Services: Design, typesetting, picture research/sourcing or original illustrations/ photography

BECKY PICKARD NM
Zebedee Design & Typesetting Services
4 Markle Steading, Nr East Linton, East Lothian, EH40 3EB
T: 07989 113 559
E: bek@zebedeedesign.co.uk; **W:** www.zebedeedesign.co.uk
Services: Internal layout and design of books up to printer-ready final pdfs; design and layout of covers and jackets from detailed brief or original concept; catalogue and brochure layout; xml into Indesign; styling and formatting of Word documents; keying; hi-res scanning; picture research

PREPRESS PROJECTS LTD NM
Algo Business Centre, Glenearn Road, Perth PH2 0NJ
T: 01738 450 490
E: enquiries@prepress-projects.co.uk; **W:** www.prepress-projects.co.uk
Services: A wide range of publishing services, including: design and typesetting; web design; print and distribution management; expert InDesign, Photoshop and Illustrator services. *See also EDITORIAL SERVICES*

REDHOUSE LANE COMMUNICATIONS NM
4TH Floor, The Hatrack, 144 St Vincent Street, Glasgow G2 5LQ
T: 0141 225 0890; **F:** 0141 225 0891
E: stephenm@redhouselane.com; **W:** www.redhouselane.com
Services: Brand origination and development, corporate publishing, design and marketing, content and editorial, internal communications consultancy, digital media strategy and design. *See also MARKETING AND PR SERVICES*

Distribution Services

BOOKSOURCE
50 Cambuslang Road, Cambuslang Investment Park, Glasgow G32 8NB
Switchboard: 0845 370 0063; **Fax**: 0845 370 0064
Credit Control: 0845 370 0065; **Fax**: 0845 370 0066
Customer Services: 0845 370 0067; **Fax**: 0845 370 0068
Email: info@booksource.net; **Website**: www.booksource.net
Established: 1995
Contacts: Louise Wilson (Client Services Manager), Davinder Bedi (Managing Director)
Services: Established in 1995, BookSource offers warehousing and worldwide distribution services to book trade publishers, charities and funded institutions and other commercial enterprises. The unique set up of BookSource, with Publishing Scotland as majority shareholder, allows for a greater amount of investment in our resources. We offer all the client services you would expect from a top-class distributor and we pride ourselves on our flexible and responsive approach. Our commitment to service is apparent in customer and client care. Many of our key personnel have been with BookSource since we started, demonstrating our commitment to our staff and their continuing enthusiasm for what we do. BookSource is committed to providing quality of delivery and service, giving our clients the competitive edge.

Editorial Services

KATE BLACKADDER NM
39 Warrender Park Terrace, Edinburgh EH9 1EB
T: 0131 228 4237
E: kate.blackadder@talk21.com
Services: Copy-editing and proofreading general non-fiction, fiction, children's books and corporate literature. Abridging books and short stories.

ALISON BOWERS
49 Mayfield Road, Edinburgh EH9 2NQ
T: 0131 667 8317
E: alibowers@blueyonder.co.uk
Services: Project editing all stages: author liaison, copy-editing, proofreading; thesis editing, student consultation. Proofreading English, French, Spanish. **Subject areas:** law, all literary/arts, history, medicine. Support and help with English presentation for visiting academics and intending authors.

BUREAUISM PUBLISHING SERVICES NM
Edinburgh, London
T: 07725 951 351
E: kirsten.campbell@bureauism.com; **W:** www.bureauism.com
Services: Editor, Project Manager and Instructional Designer, with 8 years' experience in-house and freelance, for Pearson, Cambridge University Press, EF International Language Schools, Garnet Education, LCP, etc. Complete range: project managing, editing, writing, rewriting, instructional design, podcasting, consultancy; particularly in: ELT, eLearning, young learners, education, law.

LUCY CAROLAN NM
T: 0131 228 5660
E: lucy.carolan@tiscali.co.uk
Services: Copy-editing and proofreading (non-fiction); editing for English as a second language; some specialised areas of translation (French, German and Italian)

GILLIAN CLOKE PUBLISHING SERVICES NM
16 Buckstone Close, Edinburgh EH10 6XA
T: 0131 622 0644
E: gill.cloke@virgin.net
Services: Published author, with 10 years' experience in-house and freelance, for Routledge, Elsevier, RCAHMS, EHRC, Rutland Press (now RIAS Publishing) etc. Complete range: project managing, editing, writing, rewriting, proofreading, research, reference-checking, permissions, consultancy; particularly in: education, history, medicine, religion, architecture, humanities, literature.

CHARLES COVENTRY NM
303/3 Colinton Road, Edinburgh EH13 0NR
T: 0131 441 7898
E: charlie.coventry@yahoo.co.uk
Services: Proofreading and translation into and from Gaelic for Scottish Government, Mainstream Publishing, Scottish Education Department – now Gaelic proofreader for Scottish Natural Heritage; Cassell Education (Greek), CUP Classics Division (Latin), Floris Books and private clients.

GILLIAN DAVIES NM
2a Fair-A-Far, Cramond, EH 4 6QD
T/F: 0131 336 4630; **M:** 07818 253 706
E: lawandarts@aol.com
Services: Legal and business editing, copy-writing, press release writing. See also ARTIST SERVICES.

MORVEN DOONER NM
T: 0141 423 9020; **M:** 07799 066 077
E: morven@mac.com
Services: Project management; general and structural editing of general fiction and non-fiction, reference, education; lexicography; copyediting and proofreading; editing non-native English; copywriting
Experience: 11 years' in-house publishing experience in editorial and management roles at ChambersHarrap, HarperCollins, and Neil Wilson Publishing

DUNCAN McARA

28 Beresford Gardens, Edinburgh EH5 3ES
T: 0131 552 1558
E: duncanmcara@mac.com
Services: Editorial consultant on all aspects of trade publishing. Editing, rewriting, copy-editing, proof correction for publishers, financial companies, academic institutions and other organisations. *See also* LITERARY AGENTS.

DR HELEN D McPHERSON NM

32 Restalrig Road, Edinburgh EH6 8BN
T: 0131 553 5451
E: hdmcpherson@btinternet.com
Services: Project management; editing; copy-editing; proofreading; commissioning, including multi-author/multi-volume reference works; list development and management; journal development and management; research; competitor analysis.

SUSAN MILLIGAN

39 Cecil Street (3/1), Glasgow G12 8RN
T: 0141 334 2807
E: susan@writtenword.co.uk
Services: Experienced copy-editor offering on-screen editing and proofreading general non-fiction, educational, academic and reference works, reports and company publications. Handling of illustrated non-fiction, from copy-editing to final proofs. SfEP advanced member with nine years' experience editing and/or proofreading over 120 titles. Subjects include history (ancient and modern), local history, biography and memoirs, humanities, classics, and ancient languages and civilisations.

MARY O'NEILL NM

3/1, 70 Torrisdale Street, Glasgow G42 8PJ
T: 0141 423 5019; **M**: 07765 838 095
E: mary.oneill@gmail.com
Services: Editorial project management; lexicography; copy-editing and proofreading, on screen and on hard copy. Particular experience in dictionaries, general reference, and educational publications and materials.

OSBORN EDITORIAL SERVICES **NM**

Lawrence Osborn, Flat 35, 250 Camphill Avenue, Glasgow G41 3AS
T: 0141 636 1614
E: editor@lhosborn.co.uk
Services: Copy-editing (on-screen and hard copy), proofreading, foreign language proofreading (New Testament Greek)

PAT BAXTER LANGUAGE SERVICES **NM**

104 Demondale Road, Arbroath DD11 1TW
T: 01241 875 040; **F:** 01241 875 040; **M:** 07799 761 512
E: patbaxter@btinternet.com
Services: Copy-editing (hard copy and on-screen); proofreading; rewriting; transcription. Specialist subject areas include education, accounting, languages (French, Latin), classical studies, history of art, English language/literature, general subjects; ESOL/TEFL.

PREPRESS PROJECTS LTD **NM**

Algo Business Senctre, Glenearn Road, Perth PH2 0NJ
T: 01738 450 490
E: enquiries@prepress-projects.co.uk; **W:** www.prepress-projects.co.uk
Services: A wide range of publishing services, including: publishing project management; editorial services; and print and distribution management. *See also* DESIGN SERVICES.

PROJECT ONE PUBLISHING SOLUTIONS **NM**

20 Dollerie Terrace, Crieff PH7 3EG
T: 01764 655 654
E: info@projectonepublishing.co.uk; **W:** www.projectonepublishing.co.uk
Services: As an editorial and publishing consultancy, we can offer a full range of services including: full project management (from initial concept to printer-ready files); list development; commissioning of projects; author briefing; manuscript development; writing and ghost-writing; managing and co-ordinating multi-component (print and electronic) projects; freelance design contacts; editing and proof-reading; market research and competition analysis.

RICHES EDITORIAL SERVICES
25–27 Main Street, Killearn, Glasgow G63 9RJ
T: 01360 550 544
E: info@riches-edit.co.uk; **W**: www.riches-edit.co.uk
Services: Project management, editing and proofreading, writing and updating, and commissioning and list development, with an emphasis on reference publishing, educational publishing (particularly in mathematics and science) and Scottish non-fiction publishing, based on over 30 years' full-time editorial experience with leading reference publishers. Recent projects range from editing the best-selling *The Broons' Days Oot* to updating the *Dictionary of Political Biography* for Oxford Reference Online. Clients include Birlinn, Franklin Watts, HarperCollins, Oxford University Press, Pearson Education, Times Books, Waverley Books.

ABI SAFFREY NM
E: edit@abisaffrey.co.uk; **W**: www.abisaffrey.co.uk
Services: Copy-editing and proofreading (on-screen and hard copy). I have a wide variety of experience in education (policy, guidance, teacher and student support materials), economics, ELT/EFL and politics, but will happily take on work in other social/humanities subject areas.

ANNA STEVENSON NM
T: 07747 127 296; **E**: annastevenson@hotmail.com
Qualifications and experience: MA Hons (French and German), 15 years' in-house and freelance experience. (Publishing Manager with Chambers Harrap Publishers until 2009.)
Services: publishing project management; general editing (reference, trade, academic); translation (French-English); lexicography; copy-editing; proofreading; author liaison; copywriting; non-native English. Clients include: EUP, Mainstream Publishing.

MAIRI SUTHERLAND
36 Claremont Road, Edinburgh EH6 7NH
T: 0131 555 1848
E: mairi.s@ednet.co.uk
Services: Project management; editing (hard copy and on-screen); rewriting; proofreading (hard copy and on-screen); consultancy; training. Subject areas include: arts and social science, astronomy, biography, conservation, education, geography, history, mathematics, natural history, philosophy, science, wildlife. Media: books, corporate publications (magazines, brochures, reports, annual reviews), journals, manuals, newsletters.

TOTAL PUBLISHING SOLUTIONS LTD NM
Wellbrae House, Wellbrae, Falkland KY15 7AY
T: 01337 857 097; **M:** 07855 955 517
E: susan.moody@btinternet.com
Services: Research, editing, writing, rewriting, proofreading, project
management.

TRIWORDS LTD NM
12 Sandyhill Road, Tayport, Fife DD6 9NX
T: 01382 553 172; **M:** 07990 646 864
E: kbrown@triwords.co.uk; **W:** www.triwords.co.uk
Skype: triwords
Services: On-screen and developmental editing, editing non-native English,
research and fact-checking, editorial management, website testing and
management of content, proofreading and writing services, liaison with authors.
Subjects include medical education, social sciences, policy and management.

THE TYPEHOUSE NM
25 Ramsay Drive, Dunblane FK15 0NG
T/F: 01786 823 000
E: info@thetypehouse.co.uk; **W:** thetypehouse.co.uk
Services: Publishing services for print and web including typesetting,
proofreading, copy-editing, web design and development music engraving.

GALE WINSKILL, WINSKILL EDITORIAL NM
90 Main Street, Aberdour KY3 0UH
T: 01383 860 001
E: gale@winskilleditorial.co.uk
Services: Copy-editing and proofreading (on hard copy or on-screen); workshops;
literary critiques; rewriting; editing material by non-native speakers of English;
Anglicizing or Americanizing; project management and list development.

WORDSENSE LTD NM
11 Dryden Place, Edinburgh EH9 1RP
T: 0131 667 5909
E: joannachisholm@wordsense.co.uk; **W:** www.wordsense.co.uk
Services: I am an editor, proofreader and typesetter who offers a reliable,
efficient and friendly service. My other skills are consultancy (editorial), copy-
editing, page layout, project management, research, rewriting and web page/
site content checking. I have been in business since 1981.

Indexing Services

JANE ANGUS, BSc, FGS
Darroch Den, Hawthorn Place, Ballater AB35 5QH
T: 01339 756 260
E: jane.angus@homecall.co.uk
Services: Indexing of books, journals and minutes on geology (both petroleum and environmental), natural history, the environment, agriculture and aquaculture, forestry and Scottish matters including archaeology, business and country life; also abstracting, research, proofreading and copy-editing on these topics.

ALISON BROWN
4 Allander House, Balmaha Road, Drymen, Glasgow G63 0BX
T: 01360 660 737
E: alison.brown10@virgin.net
Services: Indexing in subject fields: biography/memoirs, business/management, education, music, religion, sociology/social studies. Qualifications include the MCLIP and BIPT. Recent work has included indexing on sustainable development.

ANNE McCARTHY
Bentfield, 3 Marine Terrace, Gullane, East Lothian EH31 2AY
T/F: 01620 842 247
E: annemccarthy@btinternet.com
Services: Indexing with particular interest in medical sciences; Scottish history, language and culture; local history; sport; travel and guidebooks; biography and reference works. Over 30 years' indexing experience (MA, Fellow of Society of Indexers).

SERVICES

FRASER ROSS ASSOCIATES
6 Wellington Place, Edinburgh EH6 7EQ
T: 0131 657 4412; 0131 553 2759; F: 0131 553 2759
E: kjross@tiscali.co.uk AND lindsey.fraser@tiscali.co.uk; W: www.fraserross.co.uk
Services: Literary agency, literary consultancy and literary project management. In addition to the literary agency, which represents over 50 writers and illustrators – mainly for children, but not exclusively – Fraser Ross Associates runs The Pushkin Prizes in Scotland, a creative writing competition for pupils in S1 and S2.

JENNY BROWN ASSOCIATES **NM**
33 Argyle Place, Edinburgh EH9 1JT
T: 0131 229 5334
E: info@jennybrownassociates.co.uk; W: www.jennybrownassociates.com
Services: Scotland's largest literary agency (established 2002), representing writers of fiction (both literary and commercial), non-fiction (sport, history, biography), crime fiction and children's books. Member of Association of Authors' Agents. Please see website for submission details.

THE JUDY MOIR AGENCY **NM**
5 Gayfield Square, Edinburgh EH1 3NW
T: 0131 557 1771
E: judy_moir@blueyonder.co.uk
Services: Representing authors – adult fiction and non-fiction, with a particular emphasis on Scottish writing. Literary consultancy for publishers and other organisations.

DUNCAN McARA
28 Beresford Gardens, Edinburgh EH5 3ES
T: 0131 552 1558
E: duncanmcara@mac.com
Services: Literary agent for literary fiction; non-fiction: art, architecture, archaeology, biography, military, travel, Scottish interest. Preliminary letter with SAE essential. No reading fee. Commission: Home 15%; US/translation, film/TV 20%. See also EDITORIAL SERVICES.

THE MCKERNAN LITERARY AGENCY AND CONSULTANCY NM

5 Gayfield Square, Edinburgh EH1 3NW

T: 0131 557 1771

E: info@mckernanagency.co.uk; **W**: www.mckernanagency.co.uk

Services: Literary representation for writers, reporting and editorial services to writers and publishers.

Marketing and PR

JANE CAMILLIN NM
37 St Fillans Crescent, Aberdour, Fife, KY3 0XF
T: 07813 093 260
E: janecamillin@yahoo.co.uK
Services: Marketing plans, market research and budget planning. Catalogues, leaflets, direct mail, advanced information sheets, event management and launch events, sponsorship inquiries and applications, UK-wide media relations and publicity campaigns. Experience and advice relating to sales, key accounts, book clubs, export distribution arrangements, websites and new media. Publishing experience includes trade, fiction, reference, academic, schools and children's.

COLMAN GETTY SCOTLAND
c/o 28 Windmill Street, London W1T 2JJ
T: 020 7631 2666; **F:** 0207 631 2699
E: info@colmangetty.co.uk; **W:** www.colmangetty.co.uk
Contact: Dotti Irving
Services: UK-wide media relations, copywriting, launch events, event management, profile management. Office in London and network of associate PROs in Scotland.

REDHOUSE LANE COMMUNICATIONS NM
4TH Floor, The Hatrack, 144 St Vincent Street, Glasgow G2 5LQ
T: 0141 225 0890; **F:** 0141 225 0891
E: stephenm@redhouselane.com; **W:** www.redhouselane.com
Services: Complete end-to-end solution for clients' marketing and communication strategies. *See also* DESIGN SERVICES.

STONEHILLSALT PR
Haddington House, 28 Sidegate, Haddington, East Lothian EH41 4BU
T: 01620 829 800; **F:** 01620 829 600
E: nicky@stonehillsalt.co.uk AND rebecca@stonehillsalt.co.uk
Contacts: Rebecca Salt and Nicky Stonehill
Services: National and regional publicity campaigns, event management. Fifteen years' experience in the publishing industry and then in PR consultancy in Scotland.

Personal Focus Services

SERVICES

ORCHID (Principal: Patricia Cleghorn) **NM**
16 Tyrie Avenue, Kirkcaldy KY1 1GB
T: 01592 201 333
E: orchid2100@aol.com; **W**: www.orchidinternational.co.uk
Services: Courses, tutor training, talks, CDs and books, to help you flourish!

Photographers and Photo Libraries

CODY IMAGES
2 Reform Street, Beith, North Ayrshire KA15 2AE
T: 0845 223 5451
E: sam@codyimages.com; **W:** www.codyimages.com
Services: Specialist picture library covering aviation, warfare and transport; can
carry out picture research in these subjects. Collection includes: the history of
aviation; the exploration of space; military operations from the American Civil
War onwards; armoured fighting vehicles, weapons, equipment and warships;
transport on land and sea; personalities from aviation and military history.

GLASGOW MUSEUMS PHOTO LIBRARY
The Burrell Collection, Pollok Country Park, 2060 Pollokshaws Road,
Glasgow G43 1AT
T: 0141 287 2595; **F:** 0141 287 2585
E: photolibrary@csglasgow.org; **W:** www.glasgowmuseums.com
Services: High resolution digital images for reproduction or display of over
20,000 objects held in Glasgow City Council's 10 museums. Our knowledgeable
staff are happy to provide assistance and grant necessary permission and
licences for commercial, editorial and scholarly use of these images at very
competitive rates. Low-resolution digital images are available for personal use.

NATIONAL GALLERIES OF SCOTLAND PICTURE LIBRARY
Picture Library, Scottish National Gallery of Modern Art, 75 Belford Road,
Edinburgh EH4 3DR
T: 0131 624 6260; **F:** 0131 623 7135
E: picture.library@nationalgalleries.org; **W:** www.nationalgalleries.org
Services: The NGS Picture Library can supply photography of over 30,000
works from the national collection. We have extensive holdings of Scottish
art, surrealist works, early photography and old master paintings. The NGS
collection is now available to search online: www.nationalgalleries.org.

SANDY YOUNG
T: 07970 268 944
E: sj.young@virgin.net; **W:** www.scottishphotographer.com
Services: Award winning commercial and press photographer Sandy Young has
gained extensive experience with 14 years in the industry, leading to his current
recognised position within the media. Covering a variety of subjects ranging
from news, business and politics to arts, culture and sport, he works both in the
UK and overseas for national, regional and independent publications. To view
examples of his work visit his website.

Print and Production Services

CPI (sponsor member) **NM**
T: 01634 673 200; **Contact**: Martin McCall
E: mmccall@cpi-group.co.uk; **W**: www.cpi-group.net
Services: CPI works with a wide range of publishers and organisations. Services range from POD single-copy printing up to mass-market book production in mono and colour.

CROMWELL PRESS LTD **NM**
Aintree Avenue, White Horse Business Park, Trowbridge, Wiltshire BA14 0XB
T: 01225 711 400 **M**: 07967 591 771
E: sales@cromwellpress.co.uk; **W**: www.cromwellpress.co.uk
Services: Cromwell Press specialise in the manufacture of books, journals, loose-leaf, cased and limp mono and two-colour printing and cover jacket production

FOOTEPRINT UK **NM**
Riverside Works, Edinburgh Road, Jedburgh, Roxburghshire TD8 6AE
T: 01835 862 667; **F**: 01835 862 042
E: info@footeprint.co.uk; **W**: www.footeprint.co.uk
Services: Printing, finishing and origination for a complete range of branded business stationery.

SCA PACKAGING **NM**
166 Riverford Road, Pollokshaws, Glasgow G43 1PT
T: 0141 632 0999; **F**: 0141 632 8111
E: alan.mckinlay@sca.com; **W**: www.sca.com; Contact: Alan McKinlay
Services: SCA Packaging provides a full prepress, printing, finishing and warehouse/distribution service to its clients in several market sectors and can supply CDs/DVDs with product fulfilment, storage and distribution services.

SCOTPRINT (sponsor member) **NM**
Gateside Commerce Park, Haddington, East Lothian EH41 3ST
T: 01620 828 800; **F**: 01620 828 801; **M**: 07966 531 105
E: info@scotprint.co.uk; **W**: www.scotprint.co.uk; **Contact**: Norrie Gray
Services: Scotprint's exceptional book production facilities provide a quick route to market for a wide range of cased, sewn-limp, slotted/perfect, pur and wire-stitched books.

THOMSON LITHO LTD (sponsor member) NM
10 Colvilles Place, Kelvin Industrial Estate, East Kilbride, Glasgow G75 0SN
T: 01355 233 081; **F:** 01355 572 083; **M:** 07733 009 552
E: ycochrane@tlitho.co.uk; **W:** www.thomsonlitho.com
Services: Printing: web- and sheet-feed, monochrome, two-colour and full colour books, journals, manuals and marketing literature. Finishing: perfect binding, PUR, sewn, notch, double-wire stitching, loose-leaf, lamination, drilling, shrink-wrapping, consolidation. Optical media: CD/DVD replication. Secure storage, end user fulfilment and distribution. Please see display advert on p 167.

THOMSONLITHO

Creating the ultimate impression

Thomson Litho

Providing Printing Solutions to

Publishers for over 40 years

10 Colvilles Place, Kelvin Industrial Estate, East Kilbride, Glasgow, G75 0SN

Tel: 01355 233081

www.thomsonlitho.com

Recruitment

CITY APPOINTMENTS NM
5a Coates Place, Edinburgh, EH3 7AA
T: 0131 623 1010; **F:** 0131 623 1012
E: s.pownall@cityappointments.com; **W:** www.cityappointments.com;
Contact: Stuart Pownall
Services: City Appointments Ltd is an independent recruitment agency with over 25 years' combined experience in recruitment, including 15 years within the publishing sector.

Sales Services

BOOKSPEED
16 Salamander Yards, Edinburgh EH6 7DD
T: 0131 467 8100; **F**: 0131 467 8008
E: sales@bookspeed.com; **W**: www.bookspeed.com
Contacts: Kingsley Dawson (Managing Director), Fiona Stout (Director of Sales), Matthew Perren (Director of Buying & Logistics), Shona Rowan (Marketing & Bibliographic Manager)
Services: Supplier of books to retailers of all sizes including gift shops, museums, galleries, heritage sites and visitor attractions. Individual stock selection for customers from a database of 500,000 titles, on all subjects, at all prices, for adults and children alike.

SCOTTISH LANGUAGES DICTIONARIES NM
27 George Street, Edinburgh EH8 9LD
T/F: 0131 650 4149
Services: Advice on Scots language; courses on Scots language (CPD for teachers, librarians etc.); visits to schools, writers' groups, Burns clubs to deliver talks on Scots or lexicography; day or half-day courses on academic or business writing.

Training courses

PUBLISHING SCOTLAND
137 Dundee Street, Edinburgh EH11 1BG
T: 0131 228 6866
E: joan.lyle@publishingscotland.org; **W**: www.publishingscotland.org
The biggest provider of short publishing-related courses in Scotland. Courses
include: book and cover design, copy-editing, digital updates, marketing,
proofreading, publishing law, writing for the web and tailored in-house courses.

For Typesetting and layout services, see Design

Booksellers

Easter the Showjumper
H.M. PEEL

DISCOVERING SCOTLAND'S LOST RAILWAYS

Chambers

RCAHMS

Wanderings with a Camera in Scotland

THE GLASGOW COOKERY BOOK

a LIFE OF OSPREYS
Rou dennis

DAISYCHAIN
IN COMMAND
GJ MOFFAT

REFORMATION
HARRY REID

Mathematical Modelling for Earth Sciences
Xin-She Yang

Quick Reads
SAWBONES
STUART MACBRIDE

First Aid for Fairies and Other Fabled Beasts

101 Ways to Get Your Child to Read Patience Thomson

Collins SC
Ca

The Chambers Dictionary

DUNEDIN

Introduction

With the wealth of exciting new books published every year in Scotland, it is perhaps unsurprising that we have an abundance of well-stocked bookshops to display them all. The following list is obviously not exhaustive but it contains a good selection and covers a lot of the country. We hope to expand our listing in future editions. The stores listed alphabetically on the following pages sell books on every subject from fiction to folklore and golf to Gaelic – to find your closest shop, please see the geographical listing on pp 183–184.

Book Retailers

ACHINS BOOKSHOP
Inverkirkaig, Lochinver, Sutherland IV27 4LR
T/F: 01571 844 262
E: alex@scotbooks.freeuk.com; **W:** www.scotbooks.freeuk.com
Contact: Alex J Dickson (Partner)
Subject specialisations: Scottish; hill walking; natural history
Special services: Mail order, library and school supply

BLAST-OFF BOOKS
103 High Street, Linlithgow EH49 7EQ
T: 01506 844 645
E: info@blastoffbooks.co.uk; **W:** www.blastoffbooks.co.uk
Contact: Janet Smyth
Subject specialisations: Dedicated children's and young person's bookshop
Special services: Range of materials for youngsters with specific learning needs
eg dyslexia, autism, and ADHD. Also supply educational and general stock to
schools and libraries, organise bookfairs, author events, talks and in-service
training sessions.

BOOKSFROMSCOTLAND.COM
T: 0845 241 2779; **F:** 0131 228 3220
E: editor@booksfromscotland.com; **W:** www.booksfromscotland.com
Subject specialisations: Online bookshop and information site dedicated to
Scottish books, writers and publishers: over 14,500 books featured
Special services: Author biographies, interviews, features and essays on
Scottish books, events listings, reviews, blogs, literary maps and information on
forthcoming titles

BOTANICS SHOP
Royal Botanic Garden Edinburgh, John Hope Gateway Building, West Gate,
Arboretum Place, Edinburgh
T: 0131 552 7171
E: website form; **W:** www.rbge.org.uk
Subject specialisations: Gardening, horticultural and other books, stationery,
plants, seeds and gifts. All profits from the Botanics Shop are used directly to
support the work of the Garden.

C & E ROY

Celtic House, Bowmore, Isle of Islay, Argyll PA43 7LD
T/F: 01496 810 304
E: shop@theceltichouse.co.uk; **W**: www.theceltichouse.co.uk
Contact: Colin P Roy (Manager)
Subject specialisations: Celtic, Scottish, whisky, natural history and local interest
Special services: Mail order, customer orders

CAMPHILL BOOKSHOP

199 North Deeside Road, Bieldside, Aberdeen AB15 9EN
Open: Tues–Fri: 10am–1pm & 2pm–6pm; Sat: 10am–1pm & 2pm–5pm. Closed Sundays and Mondays. Please check times during school holidays and on Saturdays
T: 01224 867 611
Contact: Christine Thompson
Subject specialisations: Anthroposophy and biodynamics; art; childcare and development, including special needs. Children's books; cooking; craft; folklore and mythology; literature and poetry. Also stock art postcards and greetings cards.
Special services: Book tokens

THE CEILIDH PLACE BOOKSHOP

14 West Argyle Street, Ullapool, Wester Ross IV26 2TY
T: 01854 612245; **F**: 01854 613 773
E: books@theceilidhplace.com
Contact: Avril Moyes (Manager)
Subject specialisations: Scottish and international literature; poetry; politics; art; music; history; natural history; mountaineering; cookery; biography; travel writing; children's books; Gaelic; health; general fiction and general interest sections
Special services: Mail order, customer order service

THE CHILDREN'S BOOKSHOP

219 Bruntsfield Place, Edinburgh EH10 4DH
T: 0131 447 1917
E: shop@fidrabooks.co.uk; **W**: www.fidrabooks.com
Contact: Vanessa Robertson (Manager)
Subject specialisation: Children's books, with some adult stock
Special services: Book ordering and search service, school supply, author events

THE DORNOCH BOOKSHOP

High Street, Dornoch, Sutherland IV25 3SH
T: 01862 810 165; **F:** 01862 810 197
E: dornochbookshop@hotmail.com
Contact: Mrs L M Bell
Subject specialisations: Golf, Scottish, children's, general

THE EDINBURGH BOOKSHOP

181 Bruntsfield Place, Edinburgh EH10 4DG
T: 0131 229 9207
E: gallery@fidrabooks.co.uk; **W:** www.edinburghbookshop.com
Contact: Andrew Bentley-Steed (Manager)
Subject specialisation: An eclectic range of books from the classics to the quirky and from beautifully illustrated non-fiction titles to the funkiest cult novel.
Special services: Book ordering and search service; a discount for book groups, students and Society of Author members; author events

THE FOREST BOOKSHOP

26 Market Place, Selkirk TD7 4BL
E: info@theforestbookstore.co.uk
W: www.theforestbookstore.co.uk (under construction)
Contact: Allan Harkness
Core collection: Literature, Art & Environment; Contemporary & Modern fiction & poetry; Scottish & International culture, philosophy, politics
Special services: small gallery/installation space; searches & ordering (new & out of print titles)

THE LINLITHGOW BOOKSHOP

48 High Street, Linlithgow EH49 7AE
T: 01506 845 768; **F:** 01506 671 811
E: jillpattle@btinternet.com; **W:** www.linlithgowbookshop.co.uk
Contact: Jill Pattle
Subject specialisations: Eclectic range of titles, good section of local and Scottish history and a special interest in pre-school age range
Special services: Rapid ordering, extra help and advice with early years titles, loyalty schemes in all departments

NATIONAL LIBRARY OF SCOTLAND BOOKSHOP

George IV Bridge, Edinburgh, EH1 1EW
T: 0131 623 3700
E: enquiries@nls.uk; **W**: www.nls.uk/about/visitor-centre
The National Library of Scotland has new visitor facilities including a bookshop with books and other items for sale. Bookshop opening hours are: Mon-Fri: 09.30-20:00; Sat: 09.30-17.00; Sun: 14.00-17.00

RIAS BOOKSHOP

15 Rutland Square, Edinburgh EH1 2BE
Open: Mon–Fri 9am - 5 pm
T: 0131 229 7545
E: bookshop@rias.org.uk
Subject specialisations: The RIAS specialist bookshop offers the country's widest range of architecture books, technical documents and building contracts.
Special services: Online ordering through www.rias.org.uk/ebookshop.

WATERSTONE'S

W: www.waterstones.com

WATERSTONE'S SCOTTISH TEAM

Angie Crawford (Commercial Manager)
St John's Centre, Perth PH1 5UX
T: 07826 932 304
E: angie.crawford@waterstones.com

Tessa MacGregor (Marketing Manager)
98–99 Ocean Terminal, Ocean Drive, Edinburgh EH6 6JJ
T: 0131 554 4973
E: tessa.macgregor@waterstones.com

Eleanor Logan (Regional Manager West)
E: eleanor.logan@waterstones.com

Duncan Furness (Regional Manager East)
E: duncan.furness@waterstones.com

WATERSTONE'S SCOTTISH STORES

Waterstone's Aberdeen Langstane
269–271 Union Street, Aberdeen AB11 6BR
T: 01224 210 161
E: manager@aberdeen-langstane.waterstones.com

Waterstone's Aberdeen Union Bridge
3–7 Union Bridge, Trinity Centre, Aberdeen AB11 6BG
T: 01224 592 440
E: manager@aberdeen-unionbridge.waterstones.com

Waterstone's Aviemore
87 Grampian Road, Aviemore PH22 1RH
T: 01479 810 797
E: manager@aviemore.waterstones.com

Waterstone's Ayr
Unit 2, 127–147 High Street, Ayr KA7 1QR
T: 01292 262 600
E: manager@ayr.waterstones.com

Waterstone's Braehead
47 Braehead Shopping Centre, King's Inch Road, Renfrew G51 4BP
T: 0141 885 9333
E: manager@braehead.waterstones.com

Waterstone's Dumfries
79–83 High Street, Dumfries DG1 1BN
T: 01387 254 288
E: manager@dumfries.waterstones.com

Waterstone's Dundee
35 Commercial Street, Dundee DD1 3DG
T: 01382 200 322
E: manager@dundee.waterstones.com

Waterstone's Dunfermline
Unit LG17 Kingsgate Centre, Dunfermline KY12 7QU
T: 01383 720 237
E: manager@dunfermline.waterstones.com

Waterstone's East Kilbride
38a The Plaza, East Kilbride, Glasgow G74 1LW
T: 01355 271 835
E: manager@eastkilbride.waterstones.com

Waterstone's Edinburgh Cameron Toll
Cameron Toll Shopping Centre, 6 Lady Road, Edinburgh EH16 5PB
T: 0131 666 1866
E: manager@edinburgh-camerontoll.waterstones.com

Waterstone's Edinburgh East End
East End Branch, 13–14 Princes Street, Edinburgh EH2 2AN
T: 0131 556 3034/5
E: manager@edinburgh-eastend.waterstones.com

Waterstone's Edinburgh George Street
83 George Street, Edinburgh EH2 3ES
T: 0131 225 3436
E: manager@edinburgh-georgestreet.waterstones.com

Waterstone's Edinburgh Ocean Terminal
98/99 Ocean Terminal, Ocean Drive, Leith, Edinburgh EH6 6JJ
T: 0131 554 7732
E: manager@edinburgh-oceanterminal.waterstones.com

Waterstone's Edinburgh West End
128 Princes Street, Edinburgh EH2 4AD
T: 0131 226 2666
E: manager@edinburgh-westend.waterstones.com

Waterstone's Elgin
10–11 St Giles Centre, Elgin, Moray IV30 1EA
T: 01343 547 321
E: manager@elgin.waterstones.com

Waterstone's Falkirk
119–121 High Street, Falkirk FK1 1ED
T: 01324 613 116
E: manager@falkirk.waterstones.com

Waterstone's Glasgow Argyle Street
174–176 Argyle Street, Glasgow G2 8BT
T: 0141 248 4814
E: manager@glasgow-argyle.waterstones.com

Waterstone's Glasgow Sauchiehall Street
153–157 Sauchiehall Street, Glasgow G2 3EW
T: 0141 332 9105
E: manager@glasgow-sauchiehallst.waterstones.com

Waterstone's Inverness Eastgate
Unit 69, Eastgate Shopping Centre, Inverness IV2 3PR
T: 01463 233 500
E: manager@inverness-eastgatecentre.waterstones.com

Waterstone's Kirkcaldy
175 High Street, Kirkcaldy, Fife KY1 1JA
T: 01592 263 755
E: manager@kirkcaldy.waterstones.com

Waterstone's Livingston
Elements Square, The Centre, 308 Almondvale, South Livingston EH54 6GS
T: 01506 435 893
E: manager@livingston.waterstones.com

Waterstone's Newton Mearns
38 Avenue Centre, Newton Mearns, Glasgow G77 6EY
T: 0141 616 3933
E: manager@newtonmearns.waterstones.com

Waterstone's Oban
12 George Street, Oban, Argyll and Bute PA34 5SB
T: 01631 571 455
E: manager@oban.waterstones.com

Waterstone's Perth
St John's Centre, Perth PH1 5UX
T: 01738 630 013
E: manager@perth.waterstones.com

Waterstone's St Andrews
101103 Market Street, St Andrews, Fife KY16 9NX
T: 01334 477 893
E: manager@standrews.waterstones.com

Waterstone's Stirling Thistle Centre
Unit 1, Thistle Marches, Stirling FK8 2EA
T: 01786 478 756
E: manager@stirling.waterstones.com

Geographical Listing of Book Retailers

For full details, see the main Book
Retailer listings above

Aberdeen
Camphill Bookshop
Waterstone's Langstane
Waterstone's Union Bridge

Aviemore
Waterstone's Aviemore

Ayr
Waterstone's Ayr

Dornoch
The Dornoch Bookshop

Dumfries
Waterstone's Dumfries

Dundee
Waterstone's Dundee

Dunfermline
Waterstone's Dunfermline

East Kilbride
Waterstone's East Kilbride

Edinburgh
Botanics Shop
The Children's Bookshop
The Edinburgh Bookshop
National Library of Scotland Shop
RIAS Bookshop
Waterstone's Cameron Toll
Waterstone's East End
Waterstone's George Street
Waterstone's Ocean Terminal
Waterstone's West End

Elgin
Waterstone's Elgin

Falkirk
Waterstone's Falkirk

Glasgow
Waterstone's Argyle Street
Waterstone's Sauchiehall Street

Inverness
Waterstone's Eastgate

Islay
C&E Roy

Kirkcaldy
Waterstone's Kirkcaldy

Linlithgow
Blast Off Books
Linlithgow Bookshop

Livingston
Waterstone's Livingston

Lochinver
Achins Bookshop

Newton Mearns
Waterstone's Newton Mearns

Oban
Waterstone's Oban

Perth
Waterstone's Perth

Renfrew
Waterstone's Braehead

St Andrews
Waterstone's St Andrews

Selkirk
The Forest Bookshop

Stirling
Waterstone's Stirling

Ullapool
The Ceilidh Place Bookshop

Useful information

owjumper H.M. PEEL

C Collins SCOTTISH NAMES JOHN ABERNETHY

Cainnt na Caileige Caillte ALISON LANG

THE GLASGOW COOKERY BOOK

a life of ospreys roy dennis

DAISYCHAIN IN COMMAND GJ MOFFAT

REFORMATION HARRY REID

Mathematical Modelling for Earth Sciences Xin-She Yang

SMITH'S STUART MACBRIDE

Quick Reads 101 Ways to Get Your Child to Read Patience Thomson

First Aid for Fairies and Other Fabled Beasts Lari Don

WALTER SCOTT ROB ROY EDINBURGH

THE A-Z OF WHISKY GAVIN D. SMITH

NOTHING LIKE A DAME ELAINE C. SMITH

DEATH OF A LADIES' MAN ALAN BISSETT

Library Authorities in Scotland

There are 32 library authorities in Scotland responsible for hundreds of public lending libraries. Technological and other changes in recent years have led to an increase in the number of services that libraries provide including online catalogues and ordering and book reviews on their websites. Many library locations have events such as book clubs, readings, author events and some run book festivals. This list contains contact details for every library authority in Scotland. Listings for individual libraries within an authority area can be found on the authority's website.

ABERDEEN CITY COUNCIL
Library and Information Services Manager
Rosemount Viaduct, Aberdeen AB25 1GW
T: 01224 652 500; **F**: 01224 641 985; **E**: CentralLibrary@aberdeencity.gov.uk;
W: www.aberdeencity.gov.uk

ABERDEENSHIRE COUNCIL
Library and Information Services Manager
Aberdeenshire Library and Information Services Headquarters
Meldrum Meg Way, Oldmeldrum AB51 0GN
T: 01651 872 707; **E**: alis@aberdeenshire.gov.uk;
W: www.aberdeenshire.gov.uk/libraries

ANGUS COUNCIL
See website for contacts at each library
T: 08452 777 778; **E**: accessline@angus.gov.uk; **W**: www.angus.gov.uk

ARGYLL AND BUTE COUNCIL
Culture and Libraries Manager
Library Headquarters, Highland Avenue, Sandbank, Dunoon PA23 8PB
T: 01369 703 214; **F**: 01369 705 797; **W**: www.argyll-bute.gov.uk

CLACKMANNANSHIRE COUNCIL
Senior Librarian
Library Services, Alloa Library, Drysdale Street, Alloa FK10 1JL
T: 01259 450 000; **F**: 01259 219 469; **E**: libraries@clacks.gov.uk;
W: www.clacksweb.org.uk

DUMFRIES AND GALLOWAY COUNCIL
Library and Information Services Manager
Ewart Library, Dumfries DG1 1JB
T: 01387 253 820; **F:** 01387 260 294; **E:** yourlibrary@dumgal.gov.uk;
W: www.dumgal.gov.uk

DUNDEE CITY COUNCIL
Library Services Manager
Central Library, The Wellgate, Dundee DD1 1DB
T: 01382 431 500; **F:** 01382 431 558; **E:** central.library@dundeecity.gov.uk;
W: www.dundeecity.gov.uk

EAST AYRSHIRE COUNCIL
Library and Information Services Manager
Dick Institute, Elmbank Avenue, Kilmarnock KA1 3BU
T: 01563 554 300; **F:** 01563 554 311; **E:** libraries@east-ayrshire.gov.uk;
W: www.east-ayrshire.gov.uk

EAST DUNBARTONSHIRE COUNCIL
Libraries and Information Services Manager
East Dunbartonshire Libraries and Cultural Services, William Patrick Library,
2–4 West High Street, Kirkintilloch G66 1AD
T: 0141 775 4501; **F:** 0141 776 0408; **E:** libraries@eastdunbarton.gov.uk;
W: www.eastdunbarton.gov.uk

EAST LOTHIAN COUNCIL
Principal Libraries Officer
Library and Museum Headquarters, Dunbar Road, Haddington EH41 3PJ
T: 01620 828 200; **E:** libraries@eastlothian.gov.uk; **W:** www.eastlothian.gov.uk

EAST RENFREWSHIRE COUNCIL
Library Supervisor
4 Church Road, Barrhead, East Renfrewshire G78 1FA
T: 0141 577 3518; **E:** barrhead.library@eastrenfrewshire.gov.uk;
W: www.eastrenfrewshire.gov.uk

EDINBURGH CITY COUNCIL
Head of Library Services
Waverley Court, 4 East Market Street, Edinburgh EH8 8BG
T: 0131 200 2000; **F**: 0131 529 6203; **E**: eclis@edinburgh.gov.uk;
W: www.edinburgh.gov.uk

FALKIRK COUNCIL
Library Support
Victoria Buildings, Queen Street, Falkirk FK2 7AF
T: 01324 506 800; **F**: 01324 506 801; **E**: library.support@falkirk.gov.uk;
W: www.falkirk.gov.uk

FIFE COUNCIL
Libraries and Museums Manager
Central Headquarters, 16 East Fergus Place, Kirkcaldy KY1 1XT
T: 01592 583 204; **E**: libraries.museums@fife.gov.uk; **W**: www.fife.gov.uk

GLASGOW CITY COUNCIL
Libraries and Community Facilities
The Mitchell, North Street, Glasgow G3 7DN
T: 0141 287 2999; **F**: 0141 287 2815; **E**: lil@csglasgow.org; **W**: www.glasgow.gov.uk

HIGHLAND COUNCIL
Library Support Unit
3A Harbour Road, Inverness IV1 1UA
T: 01463 235 713; **E**: libraries@highland.gov.co.uk; **W**: www.highland.gov.uk

INVERCLYDE COUNCIL
Head of Library Services
Central Library, Clyde Square, Greenock PA15 1NA
T: 01475 712 323; **F**: 01475 712 334; **E**: library.central@inverclyde.gov.uk;
W: www.inverclyde.gov.uk

MIDLOTHIAN COUNCIL
Library Services Manager
Library Headquarters, 2 Clerk Street, Loanhead EH20 9DR
T: 0131 271 3980; **F**: 0131 440 4635; **E**: library.hq@midlothian.gov.uk;
W: www.midlothian.gov.uk

MORAY COUNCIL
Libraries and Museums Manager
High Street, Elgin, Moray IV30 1BX
T: 01343 563 398; **F**: 01343 563 478; **E**: librarymanager@moray.gov.uk;
W: www.moray.gov.uk

NORTH AYRSHIRE COUNCIL
Head of Library Services
Cunninghame House, Friarscroft, Irvine KA12 8EE
T: 0845 603 0590; **F**: 01294 324 144; **E**: libraryhq@north-ayrshire.gov.uk;
W: www.north-ayrshire.gov.uk

NORTH LANARKSHIRE COUNCIL
Library Supervisor
Libraries and Information, Stepps Cultural Centre, 10 Blenheim Ave,
Stepps G33 6FH
T: 01236 638 555; **E**: via contact form on website; **W**: www.northlan.gov.uk

ORKNEY ISLANDS COUNCIL
Library and Archive Manager
Orkney Islands Council Libraries, 44 Junction Road, Kirkwall, Orkney KW15 1AG
T: 01856 873 166; **F**: 01865 875 260; **E**: general.enquiries@orkneylibrary.org.uk;
W: www.orkney.gov.uk

PERTH AND KINROSS COUNCIL
Head of Cultural and Community Services
Puller House, 35 Kinnoull Street, Perth PH1 5GD
T: 01738 476 200; **E**: library@pkc.gov.uk; **W**: www.pkc.gov.uk

RENFREWSHIRE COUNCIL
Central Library, 68 High Street, Paisley PA1 2BB
T: 0141 889 2360; **F**: 0141 887 6468; **E**: ref.els@renfrewshire.gov.uk;
W: www.renfrewshire.gov.uk

SCOTTISH BORDERS COUNCIL
Libraries and Information Services Manager
Library HQ, St Mary's Mill, Selkirk TD7 5EW
T: 01750 20842; **F**: 01750 22875; **W**: www.scotborders.gov.uk

SHETLAND ISLANDS COUNCIL
Library and Information Services Manager
Shetland Library, Lower Hillhead, Lerwick Shetland ZE1 0EL
T: 01595 743 868; **F**: 01595 694 430; **E**: shetlandlibrary@sic.shetland.gov.uk;
W: www.shetland.gov.uk

SOUTH AYRSHIRE COUNCIL
Library Services
Carnegie Library, 12 Main Street, Ayr KA8 8EB
T: 01292 286 385; **W**: www.south-ayrshire.gov.uk/libraries

SOUTH LANARKSHIRE COUNCIL
Library Services Manager
Council Headquarters, Almada Street, Hamilton ML3 0AE
T: 01698 454 412; **F**: 01698 454 398; **W**: www.southlanarkshire.gov.uk

STIRLING COUNCIL
Head of Libraries Heritage and Cultural Services
6 Borrowmeadow Road, Springkerse Industrial Estate, Stirling FK7 7TN
T: 01786 432 383; **F**: 01786 432 395; **E**: libraryheadquarters@stirling.gov.uk;
W: www.stirling.gov.uk

WEST DUNBARTONSHIRE COUNCIL
Senior Librarian
19 Poplar Road, Broadmeadow Industrial Estate, Dumbarton G82 2RJ
T: 01389 737 000; **E**: library.headquarters@west-dunbarton.gov.uk;
W: www.wdcweb.info/arts-culture-and-libraries/libraries

WEST LOTHIAN COUNCIL
Library Services Manager
Connolly House, Hopefield Road, Blackburn EH47 7HZ
T: 01506 776 336; **F**: 01506 776 345; **E**: library.info@westlothian.gov.uk;
W: www.wlonline.org

WESTERN ISLES COUNCIL
Chief Librarian
Sandwick Road, Stornoway, Isle of Lewis HS1 2BW
T: 01851 703 773; **F**: 01851 705 349; **E**: enquiries@cne-siar.gov.uk;
W: www.cne-siar.gov.uk/library

Organisations: list of useful addresses

The following list contains organisations of interest to those in publishing and areas related to it. Additional sources of information may be found in the list of Resources on pp 203–207.

AGENTS

ASSOCIATION OF AUTHORS' AGENTS
Anthony Goff, c/o David Higham Associates Ltd, 5-8 Lower John Street, Golden Square, London W1F 9HA; **T**: 0207 7434 5900;
E: anthonygoff@davidhigham.co.uk; **W**: www.agentsassoc.co.uk
A forum for member agents to discuss industry matters, to uphold a code of good practice and to represent the interests of authors and agents.

ARCHIVES

EDINBURGH CITY OF PRINT
SCOB, Edinburgh Napier University, Craighouse Campus, Edinburgh EH10 5LG
T: 0131 455 6465; **F**: 0131 455 6306; **E**: sapphire@napier.ac.uk;
W: www.edinburghcityofprint.org
Edinburgh City of Print is a joint project between the City of Edinburgh Museums and Galleries and the Scottish Archive of Print and Publishing History Records (SAPPHIRE). The project aims to catalogue and make accessible the wealth of printing collections held by City of Edinburgh Museums and Galleries.

SCOTTISH ARCHIVE OF PRINT AND PUBLISHING HISTORY RECORDS (SAPPHIRE)
SCOB, Edinburgh Napier University, Craighouse Campus, Edinburgh EH10 5LG
T: 0131 455 6465; **F**: 0131 455 6306; **E**: sapphire@napier.ac.uk;
W: www.sapphire.ac.uk
SAPPHIRE aims to record the social, economic and cultural history of the Scottish printing and publishing industries.

SCOTTISH PRINTING ARCHIVAL TRUST
3 Zetland Place, Edinburgh EH5 3HU
T: 0131 552 2596; **E**: b.clegg@scottishprintarchive.org;
W: www.scottishprintarchive.org
Records information, institutes research and acquires material relating to the development of Scottish printing for the benefit of the public and print media education.

ARTS AND CULTURE

BRITISH COUNCIL
The Tun, 4 Jackson's Entry, Holyrood Road, Edinburgh EH8 8PJ
T: 0131 524 5700; **F**: 0131 524 5701; **E**: scotland.enquiries@britishcouncil.org;
W: www.britishcouncil.org
The British Council is the United Kingdom's international organisation for
educational opportunities and cultural relations. Its purpose is to build mutually
beneficial relationships between people in the UK and other countries and to
increase appreciation of the UK's creative ideas and achievements.

CREATIVE SCOTLAND
E: via form on website; **W**: www.creativescotland.org.uk
Creative Scotland the statutory non-departmental public body (NDPB) is
expected to be formally established in 2010. It is the new organisation tasked
with leading the development of the arts, creative and screen industries across
Scotland and will replace the Scottish Arts Council and Scottish Screen.

SCOTTISH ARTS COUNCIL
12 Manor Place, Edinburgh EH3 7DD
T: 0131 226 6051; **T** (Helpdesk): 0845 603 6000; **F**: 0131 225 9833;
E: help.desk@scottisharts.org.uk; **W**: www.scottisharts.org.uk
The Scottish Arts Council champions the arts for Scotland. Its main aims are to
increase participation in the arts; to support artists in fulfilling their creative and
business potential; and to place arts, culture and creativity at the heart of learning.

AUTHORS

ALCS (THE AUTHORS' LICENSING AND COLLECTING SOCIETY)
The Writers' House, 13 Haydon Street, London, EC3N 1DB
T: 0207 264 5700; **F**: 0207 264 5755; **E**: alcs@alcs.co.uk; **W**: www.alcs.co.uk
The Authors' Licensing and Collecting Society (ALCS) represents the interests of
all UK writers and aims to ensure writers are fairly compensated for any works
that are copied, broadcast or recorded.

LITERATURETRAINING
Literaturetraining, PO Box 23595, Leith EH6 7YX
T: 0131 553 2210; **E**: info@literaturetraining.com; **W**: www.literaturetraining.com
literaturetraining acts a first stop shop for writers and literature professionals
across the UK looking for information and advice that will help them to move

forward professionally. It is a wing of the National Association of Writers in Education and is run in conjunction with its other partner literature organisations Academi, Apples & Snakes, Lapidus, NALD, renaissance one, Scottish Book Trust, Survivors Poetry and writernet.

THE SCOTTISH ASSOCIATION OF WRITERS
W: www.sawriters.org.uk; **Contact**: Marc R Sherland (Secretary)
E: marcsherland@btinternet.com
The Scottish Association of Writers has over 30 clubs affiliated to it. It promotes and encourages the art and craft of writing in all its forms; promotes and runs weekend schools and conferences for members; and promotes and encourages participation in competitions in various forms of writing.

SOCIETY OF AUTHORS IN SCOTLAND NM
Caroline Dunford (Honorary Secretary), 17 Pittville St Lane, Edinburgh EH15 2BU
T: 0131 657 1391; **E**: verdandiweaves@mac.com; **W**: www.societyofauthors.net
The Society of Authors (HQ 84 Drayton Gardens, London SW10 9SB) is an independent trade union, representing writers' interests in all aspects of the writing profession and has over 500 members in Scotland.

BIBLIOGRAPHIC INFORMATION

BDS (BIBLIOGRAPHIC DATA SERVICES)
Bibliographic Data Services Limited, Annandale House, The Crichton, Dumfries DG1 4TA
W: www.bibliographicdata.com
BDS is the premier source of industry-standard information on book publications and home entertainment releases. BDS offers libraries, publishers and booksellers the data solution they need to remain efficient, cost-effective and up to date.

COMPANIES UNDER THE NIELSEN BOOKDATA UMBRELLA
Nielsen BookData
3rd Floor, Midas House, 62 Goldsworth Road, Woking GU21 6LQ
T: 01483 712 200; **F**: 01483 712 201; **E**: sales.bookdata@nielsen.com;
W: www.nielsenbookdata.co.uk
Provides booksellers and librarians with the most up-to-date, timely, accurate and content-rich book information for all English-language books (and other published media, including e-books), published internationally.

ORGANISATIONS: LIST OF USEFUL ADDRESSES

193

BookNet (Transaction Services)
3rd Floor, Midas House, 62 Goldsworth Road, Woking GU21 6LQ
T: 01483 712 200; **F:** 01483 712 201; **E:** sales.booknet@nielsen.com;
W: www.nielsenbooknet.co.uk
Provides e-commerce to the industry that delivers a means of efficient
and cost-effective trading between partners regardless of size or location.

Nielsen BookScan
3rd Floor, Midas House, 62 Goldsworth Road, Woking GU21 6LQ
T: 01483 712 222; **F:** 01483 712 220; **E:** sales.bookscan@nielsen.com;
W: www.nielsenbookscan.co.uk
Provides online, actionable, business-critical sales information to the industry

UK Registration Agencies operated by Nielsen BookData
3rd Floor, Midas House, 62 Goldsworth Road, Woking GU21 6LQ
T: 0870 777 8712; **F:** 0870 777 8714; **E:** isbn.agency@nielsen.com; san.agency@
nielsen.com; istc.agency@nielsen.com; **W:** www.isbn.nielsenbookdata.co.uk;
www.san.nielsenbook.co.uk; www.istc.nielsenbook.co.uk
Nielsen BookData Registration Services provide UK and other English-language
publishers with a range of standard identifiers for use in the international supply
chain. The ISBN Agency issues ISBNs to publishers based in the UK and the
Republic of Ireland (can provide help and advice on changing from ten to 13 digits).
The SAN Agency is administered on behalf of the Book Industry Communication.
It assigns Standard Address Numbers and Global Location Numbers for
organisations in any country except USA, Canada, Australia and New Zealand.
Nielsen Book operates one of the first ISTC Registration Agencies, enabling
authors, publishers and other authorised representatives to register textual
works with an ISTC (the International Standard Text Code is a global identification
system for textual works, ie the 'content' in text-based publications).

BLIND (SERVICES FOR THE)

RNIB SCOTLAND TRANSCRIPTION CENTRE
RNIB Scotland: Transcription Service, Centre for Sensory Impaired People,
17 Gullane Street, Glasgow G11 6AH
T: 0141 337 2955; **F:** 0141 357 4025; **E:** glasgowtrans@rnib.org.uk;
W: www.rnib.org.uk
RNIB Scotland is the leading charity working with blind and partially sighted
people in Scotland. The RNIB's Transcription Centre converts print and other
material into formats which blind and partially sighted people can read.

SCOTTISH BRAILLE PRESS

Craigmillar Park, Edinburgh EH16 5NB
T: 0131 662 4445; **F**: 0131 662 1968; **E**: enquiries.sbp@royalblind.org;
W: www.royalblind.org/sbp/
Since its establishment in 1891, the Scottish Braille Press has grown to become one of the world's leading producers of reading material for blind people.

BOOKSELLING

BOOKSELLERS ASSOCIATION OF THE UNITED KINGDOM AND IRELAND LTD

Minster House, 272 Vauxhall Bridge Road, London SW1V 1BA
T: 0207 802 0802; **F**: 0207 802 0803; **E**: mail@booksellers.org.uk; **W**: www. booksellers.org.uk
A trade association representing 95% of booksellers in the UK and Ireland, it promotes bookselling through lobbying, campaigning and provision of events, and access to a range of services and products.

CHILDREN

FEDERATION OF CHILDREN'S BOOK GROUPS

c/o Martin and Sinéad Kromer, 2 Bridge Wood View, Horsforth, Leeds, West Yorkshire LS18 5PE
E: via form on website; **W**: www.fcbg.org.uk
A voluntary organisation for parents, teachers, librarians, booksellers, publishers and all who are interested in books and children from 0–16 years. Local activities range from talks, book sales, Family Reading Groups and story times to sponsored author visits and out-of-school fun events. National events include booklists, National Share-a-Story Month and annual conferences.

SCWBI SCOTLAND (SOCIETY OF CHILDREN'S BOOK WRITERS AND ILLUSTRATORS)

The Society of Children's Book Writers and Illustrators is an international organisation that acts as a network for the exchange of knowledge between writers, illustrators, editors, publishers, agents, librarians, educators, booksellers and others involved with literature for young people. The Regional Advisor for Scotland is author Claira Jo.
E: ra@scbwiscotland.co.uk; **W**: www.scbwiscotland.co.uk

COPYRIGHT

ALCS, see **Authors** above

THE COPYRIGHT LICENSING AGENCY LTD
CBC House, 24 Canning Street, Edinburgh EH3 8EG
T: 0131 272 2711; **F:** 0131 272 2811; **E:** clascotland@cla.co.uk; **W:** www.cla.co.uk
and Saffron House, 6–10 Kirby St, London EC1N 8TS
T: 0207 400 3100; **F:** 0207 400 3101; **E:** cla@cla.co.uk
The Copyright Licensing Agency (CLA) is a single source for the authorisation
of copying and to establish and manage licensing schemes for institutional and
professional organisations where extensive photocopying of books, journals and
periodicals occurs.

DRAMA

PLAYWRIGHTS' STUDIO, SCOTLAND
CCA, 350 Sauchiehall Street, Glasgow G2 3JD
T: 0141 332 4403; **E:** info@playwrightsstudio.co.uk;
W: www.playwrightsstudio.co.uk
Playwrights' Studio, Scotland is a national organisation which directly engages
the people of Scotland with new playwriting and raises the standard of plays for
presentation to the public.

EDITORIAL AND PROOFREADING

SOCIETY FOR EDITORS AND PROOFREADERS (SFEP)
Erico House, 93-99 Upper Richmond Road, Putney, London, SW15 2TG
T: 020 8785 5617; **F:** 020 8785 5618; **E:** administration@sfep.org.uk;
W: www.sfep.org.uk
Promotes high editorial standards and achieves recognition of the professional
status of its members.

SOCIETY FOR EDITORS AND PROOFREADERS – GLASGOW GROUP
E: glasgow@sfep.org.uk; **W:** www.sfep-glasgow.org.uk
The Glasgow SfEP group is a loose coalition of diverse professionals, all
members or associates of the Society for Editors and Proofreaders, who share
a belief in editorial excellence and the importance of being in touch with like-
minded people.

EDUCATION

LEARNING AND TEACHING SCOTLAND
The Optima Building, 58 Robertson Street, Glasgow G2 8DU
T: 0141 282 5000 (Reception); **F**: 0141 282 5050; **E**: enquiries@LTScotland.org.uk;
W: www.ltscotland.org.uk
Learning and Teaching Scotland (LTS) provides advice, support, resources and
staff development to the education community, creating a culture of innovation,
ambition and excellence throughout Scottish education.

SCOTTISH QUALIFICATIONS AUTHORITY
The Optima Building, 58 Robertson Street, Glasgow G2 8DQ
T: 0845 279 1000; **F**: 0845 213 5000; **E**: customer@sqa.org.uk; **W**: www.sqa.org.uk
SQA is an executive non-departmental public body (NDPB) sponsored by the
Scottish Government Schools Directorate. It is the national body in Scotland
responsible for the development, accreditation, assessment and certification of
qualifications other than degrees.

GAELIC

COMHAIRLE NAN LEABHRAICHEAN/ THE GAELIC BOOKS COUNCIL **PS**
22 Mansfield Street, Glasgow G11 5QP
T: 0141 337 6211; **F**: 0141 341 0515; **E**: brath@gaelicbooks.net;
W: www.gaelicbooks.org
A charitable company whose purpose is to assist and stimulate Gaelic
publishing.

INDEXERS

SOCIETY OF INDEXERS (SCOTTISH GROUP)
E: scotland@indexers.org.uk; **W**: www.indexers.org.uk
The Scottish group represents the Society locally. It aims to promote indexing
amongst Scottish publishers and authors and to provide a forum for indexers.

LEGAL DEPOSIT

NATIONAL LIBRARY OF SCOTLAND
The Legal Deposit Team, Modern British Collections Unit, National Library of
Scotland, 33 Salisbury Place, Edinburgh EH9 1SL
T: 0131 623 4661 (print enquiries); 0131 623 4671 (non-print enquiries);
E: legal-deposit-enquiries@nls.uk; **W**: www.nls.uk/about/legaldeposit/
The National Library is a Legal Deposit library, and is therefore entitled to claim
copies of every printed book published in the UK and Ireland. The Code of
Practice for the Voluntary Deposit of Non-Print Publications, implemented from
the beginning of 2000, means that the Library can request the deposit of some
categories of non-print material. Full details can be found on its website at www.
nls.uk/about/legaldeposit/.

LIBRARIES

CILIPS (formerly Scottish Library Association) **PS**
1st Floor Building C, Brandon Gate, Leechlee Road, Hamilton ML3 6AU
T: 01698 458 888; **F**: 01698 283 170; **E**: cilips@slainte.org.uk;
W: www.slainte.org.uk
The Chartered Institute of Library and Information Professionals in Scotland
(CILIPS), was formed in 2002 by the amalgamation of the Library Association
and the Institute of Information Scientists. CILIPS works on behalf of Scottish
members to improve and support Scottish library and information services.

LOCAL AUTHORITY LIBRARIES, see pp 185–191 above.

NATIONAL LIBRARY OF SCOTLAND **PS**
George IV Bridge, Edinburgh EH1 1EW
T: 0131 623 3700; **F**: 0131 623 3701; **W**: www.nls.uk
The National Library of Scotland is a reference library with world-class
collections. NLS is also Scotland's largest library and one of the major research
libraries in Europe. Being a Legal Deposit library, it is entitled to claim copies of
every book published in the UK and Ireland (*see* LEGAL DEPOSIT *above*).

SCHOOL LIBRARY ASSOCIATION (SCOTLAND)
Convenor: Duncan Wright; **T**: 0131 311 1065; **E**: swrightd@esmgc.com;
W: www.sla.org.uk/branch-scotland.php
Secretary: Rebecca Christine; **T**: 0131 347 5766; **E**: schristiner@esmgc.com
The School Library Association (Scotland) is a branch of the School Library

Association which supports all those committed to the promotion and development of school libraries and information literacy. The Association in Scotland usually holds training days.

SCOTTISH POETRY LIBRARY
5 Crichton's Close, Canongate, Edinburgh EH8 8DT
T: 0131 557 2876; **F**: 0131 557 8393; **E**: reception@spl.org.uk; **W**: www.spl.org.uk
The Scottish Poetry Library (SPL), a registered charity open since February 1984, aims to make the poetry of Scotland – in whatever language – and a selection of mainly modern poetry from other countries, visible and freely accessible to the general public throughout the country.

SLIC
1st Floor Building C, Brandon Gate, Leechlee Road, Hamilton ML3 6AU
T: 01698 458 888; **F**: 01698 283 170; **E**: slic@slainte.org.uk; **W**: www.slainte.org.uk
The Scottish Library and Information Council (SLIC) is the independent advisory body to the Scottish Government and Scottish ministers on library and information matters. SLIC members include all local authority, higher education, further education organisations, NHS Trust library services, as well as other specialist library and information organisations.

LITERARY

ASSOCIATION FOR SCOTTISH LITERARY STUDIES PS
c/o Department of Scottish Literature, University of Glasgow,
7 University Gardens, Glasgow G12 8QH
T: 0141 330 5309; **E**: office@asls.org.uk; **W**: www.asls.org.uk
The Association for Scottish Literary Studies (ASLS) exists to promote the study, teaching and writing of Scottish literature and to further the study of the languages of Scotland.

EDINBURGH UNESCO CITY OF LITERATURE
The Edinburgh Room, Central Library, George IV Bridge, Edinburgh EH1 1EG
T: 0131 220 2970; **W**: www.cityofliterature.com
In October 2004 Edinburgh became the first UNESCO City of Literature in the world. The designation serves as global recognition of Edinburgh's rich literary heritage, thriving contemporary scene and bold aspirations for the future. The permanent award has concentrated efforts to attract new literary initiatives to Scotland while enabling the development with future international cities of literature to establish a world wide network.

SCOTTISH BOOK TRUST [PS]

Sandeman House, Trunk's Close, 55 High Street, Edinburgh EH1 1SR
T: 0131 524 0160; **F:** 0131 524 0161; **E:** info@scottishbooktrust.com;
W: www.scottishbooktrust.com
Scottish Book Trust is Scotland's national agency for readers and writers. It runs a range of programmes and projects that encourage an enjoyment and engagement with books, authors, reading and writing.

SCOTTISH POETRY LIBRARY, see *LIBRARIES*

NEWSPAPERS

SCOTTISH DAILY NEWSPAPER SOCIETY, THE

21 Lansdowne Crescent, Edinburgh EH12 5EH
T: 0131 535 1064; **F:** 0131 535 1063; **E:** info@sdns.org.uk
Promotes and represents the interests of publishers of Scottish daily and Sunday newspapers.

PRINT

SCOTTISH PRINT EMPLOYERS FEDERATION

48 Palmerston Place, Edinburgh EH12 5DE
T: 0131 220 4353; **F:** 0131 220 4344; **E:** info@spef.org.uk; **W:** www.spef.org.uk
The Federation is the employers' organisation/trade association for all sectors of the printing industry in Scotland and promotes and represents the interests of the Scottish printing industry.

SCOTTISH PRINTING ARCHIVAL TRUST, see *ARCHIVES*

PROOFREADING, SEE EDITORIAL AND PROOFREADING

PUBLIC LENDING RIGHT

PUBLIC LENDING RIGHT

Richard House, Sorbonne Close, Stockton-on-Tees TS17 6DA
T: 01642 604 699; **F:** 01642 615 641; **E:** via form on website; **W:** www.plr.uk.com
The Public Lending Right legislation gives authors a statutory right to receive payment for the free lending of their books from public libraries throughout the UK. PLR is administered by the Registrar and his staff whose function is to collect loans data and make payments to registered authors on the basis of how often their books are borrowed.

PUBLISHING

ALPSP
W: www.alpsp.org
The Association of Learned and Professional Society Publishers (ALPSP) is the only international trade association representing all types of nonprofit publishers, and is the largest trade association for scholarly and professional publishers.

AOP
Queens House, 55/56 Lincolns Inn Fields, Holborn, London WC2A 3LJ
T: 0207 404 4166; **F**: 0207 404 4167; **E**: info@ukaop.org.uk; **W**: www.ukaop.org.uk
The UK Association of Online Publishers (AOP) is an industry body representing digital publishing companies that create original, branded, quality content.

INDEPENDENT PUBLISHERS GUILD
PO Box 12, Llain, Whitland SA34 0WU
T: 01437 563 335; **F**: 01437 562 071; **E**:info@ipg.uk.com; **W**: www.ipg.uk.com
The Independent Publishers Guild (IPG) is an association for independent publishers.

PPA SCOTLAND
Kathy Crawford, Business Manager, 22 Rhodes Park, Tantallon Road, North Berwick EH39 5NA
T: 01620 890 800; **W**: www.ppa.co.uk
PPA Scotland is the Scottish arm of the Periodical Publishers Association (see *PPA and its members* area of the PPA website).

THE PUBLISHERS ASSOCIATION
29b Montague Street, London WC1B 5BW
T: 0207 691 9191; **F**: 0207 691 9199; **E**: mail@publishers.org.uk;
W: www.publishers.org.uk
The Publishers Association is the leading trade organisation serving book, journal and electronic publishers in the UK.

PUBLISHING IRELAND (formerly CLÉ)
Guinness Enterprise Centre, Taylor's Lane, Dublin 8
T: 00 353 (0)1 415 1210; **E**: info@publishingireland.com;
W: www.publishingireland.com
Publishing Ireland is the Irish Book Publishers' Association. It is a cross-border organisation and membership comprises most of the major publishing houses in Ireland with a mixture of trade, general and academic publishers as members.

PUBLISHING SCOTLAND
The Scottish Book Centre, 137 Dundee Street, Edinburgh EH11 1BG
T: 0131 228 6866; **F:** 0131 228 3220; **E:** enquiries@publishingscotland.org;
W: www.publishingscotland.org
Publishing Scotland is a not-for-profit company, formed to take responsibility
for the representation and development of the publishing sector in Scotland. It
acts as the voice and network for publishing, to develop and promote the work
of companies, organisations and individuals in the industry, and to co-ordinate
joint initiatives and partnership.

SCOTTISH CENTRE FOR THE BOOK (SCOB)
Napier University, Craighouse Campus, Edinburgh EH10 5LG
T: 0131 455 6429; **F:** 0131 455 6193; **E:** scob@napier.ac.uk;
W: www.scob.org.uk, www.napier.ac.uk/scob
The Scottish Centre for the Book acts as a focus for research and knowledge
transfer in publishing and the material book.

SOCIETY OF YOUNG PUBLISHERS IN SCOTLAND
8/2 Edina Street, Edinburgh EH7 5PN.
T: 0797 426 1567 (Dayspring MacLeod, chair) **E:** scotland@thesyp.org.uk
W: www.thesyp.org.uk
The Society of Young Publishers is a UK-wide network for those who work in
publishing or wish to join the field. The Scottish chapter is based in Edinburgh
but will run events throughout the country. SYP holds speaker meetings and
social networking events, as well as supporting members through newsletters
and web-based updates.

THE WELSH BOOKS COUNCIL
Welsh Books Council, Castell Brychan, Aberystwyth, Ceredigion SY23 2JB
T: 01970 624151; **F:** 01970 625385; **E:** castellbrychan@wbc.org.uk;
W: www.cllc.org.uk
The Welsh Books Council is a national body, funded by the Welsh Assembly
Government, which provides a focus for the publishing industry in Wales.

WRITERS, see AUTHORS above

Resources

This list of resources contains useful books and other resources of interest to those in the business of publishing. Books marked * can be consulted at or borrowed from Publishing Scotland's Resource Library. The library contains other reference books of interest to members as well as trade journal *The Bookseller* and other magazines and journals.

ACQUISITION AND COMMISSIONING
Davies, Gill *Book Commissioning and Acquisition* (London: Routledge, 2004)

BOOK FAIRS
For a list of the main book fairs, see www.publishingscotland.org
London International Book Fair (19–21 April 2010): www.londonbookfair.co.uk
BookExpo America (25–27 May 2010 in New York): www.bookexpoamerica.com
Frankfurt Book Fair (6–10 October 2010): www.buchmesse.de.en

BOOK TRADE INFORMATION
PA Book Trade Yearbook 1990-2007 (London: Publishers Association, Annual)*
Website and email updates on book trade information: see www.booktrade.info

BUSINESS AND FINANCIAL ASPECTS OF PUBLISHING
Bellaigue, Eric de *British Book Publishing as a Business Since the 1960s* (London: The British Library, 2004)
Epstein, Jason *Book Business: Publishing Past, Present and Future* (London: WW Norton & Co, 2002)
Greco, Albert N *The Book Publishing Industry* (London: Lawrence Erlbaum Associates, 2004)
Miller, Laura *Reluctant Capitalists: Bookselling and the Culture of Consumption* (London: The University of Chicago Press, 2007)
Woll, T and Nathan, J *Publishing for Profit: Successful Bottom-Line Management for Book Publishers* (Chicago: Chicago Review Press, 2006) (New edition due January 2010)

CAREERS IN PUBLISHING
Baverstock, A, et al *How to Get a Job in Publishing: A Really Practical Guide to Careers in Books and Magazines* (London: A & C Clarke Publishers Ltd, 2008)
For advertised publishing vacancies, the main sources are the *Guardian* newspaper and website (www.jobs.guardian.co.uk), and the *Bookseller* weekly magazine and its website (www.bookseller.com). Publishing organisations (including Publishing Scotland: www.publishingscotland.org), universities with publishing courses and of course the publishers themselves may also advertise jobs and work experience opportunities on their websites.

The Graduate Careers website has useful job descriptions of typical jobs in
   publishing: see www.prospects.ac.uk
The National Occupational Standards for Publishing provide detailed
   descriptions of publishing job competencies: see www.train4publishing.co.uk

COPYRIGHT, CONTRACTS AND RIGHTS

Jones, H and Benson, C Publishing Law (3rd edn, 2006: London, Routledge)
Owen, Lynette (ed) Clark's Publishing Agreements: A Book of Precedents (Tottel
   Publishing, 2007)*
Owen, Lynette Selling Rights (London: Routledge, 2006) (New edition due July
   2010)
Society of Authors (www.societyofauthors.org)
UK Intellectual Property Office (www.ipo.gov.uk)
Copyright Licensing Agency (www.cla.co.uk)

DESIGN AND TYPOGRAPHY

Baines, P and Haslam, A Type & Typography (2nd edn, 2005: Watson-Guptill
   Publications)*
Birdsall, Derek Notes on Book Design (Yale University Press, 2004)*
Sutton, J and Bartram, A Typefaces for Books (British Library Publishing Division,
   1990)*
Williams, R The Non-Designer's Design Book (3rd edn, 2008: Peachpit Press)
The premier book design awards in the UK are the British Book Design and
   Production Awards (see www.britishbookawards.org)

DIRECTORIES AND YEARBOOKS

Publishing Scotland Yearbook (Edinburgh: Publishing Scotland, Annual)
Writers' and Artists' Yearbook (London: A & C Black, Annual)

EDITING AND INDEXING

Butcher, J, Drake, C and Leach, M Butcher's Copy-editing: The Cambridge Handbook
   for Editors, Copy-editors and Proofreaders (4th edn, 2006, Cambridge University
   Press)
Gross, Gerald Editors on Editing (New York, Grove Press, 2000)
Horn, Barbara Editorial Project Management (Horn Editorial Books, 2006)
Ritter, R M New Hart's Rules (Oxford University Press, 2005)

E-PUBLISHING

Arms, W Digital Libraries and Electronic publishing (MIT Press, 2001)
Austin, T and Doust, R New Media Design (Laurence King, 2007)

Bergsland, D *Introduction to Digital Publishing* (Thomson Delmar Learning, 2002)
Curtis, R and Quick, WT *How to Get Your E-Book Published: An Insider's Guide to the World of Electronic Publishing* (F&W Pubns, 2002)

RESOURCES

INTRODUCTION TO PUBLISHING
Clark, Giles and Phillips, A *Inside Book Publishing* (4th edn, London: Routledge, 2008)*
Feather, John *A History of British Publishing* (London: Routledge, 2005)
Richardson, P and Taylor, G *A Guide to the UK Publishing Industry* (London: Publishers Association, 2008)

MARKETING
Baverstock, Alison *How to Market Books: The Essential Guide to Maximizing Profit and Exploiting All Channels to Market* (4th edn, 2008, London: Kogan Page)
Rosenthal, Morris *Print-On-Demand Book Publishing: A New Approach to Printing and Marketing Books for Publishers and Authors* (Springfield, Mass: Foner Books, 2004)
BML. BML is the premier source of information and research on the book industry, undertaking a wide range of private and syndicated research projects, and publishing a variety of market reports. Its continuous survey, *Books and the Consumer* provides detailed information on British book buying behaviour: see www.bookmarketing.co.uk.

PRINT AND PRODUCTION
Bann, D *The All New Print Production Handbook* (PIRA : 2007)
Marshall, L *Bookmaking, Editing/Design/Production* (3rd revised edn, 2009: W W Norton & Co)

PUBLISHERS
Publishers in Scotland. Members of Publishing Scotland are listed in its annual directory *Publishing Scotland Yearbook* which also lists other publishers in Scotland.
Publishers in Scotland. Members of Publishing Scotland are listed on its website: www.publishingscotland.org
Publishers outside of Scotland. See the websites of publisher member organisations (the main UK and Irish ones are listed under Organisations)
Scottish Book Trade Index (SBTI). The Scottish Book Trade Index represents an index of printers, publishers, booksellers, bookbinders, printmakers, stationers and papermakers based in Scotland, from the beginnings of Scottish printing to about 1850. It is compiled and maintained by the National Library of Scotland: see www.nls.uk.

QUALIFICATIONS
EDINBURGH NAPIER UNIVERSITY
School of Arts & Creative Industries, Craighouse Campus, Craighouse Road, Edinburgh EH10 5LG
T: 0131 455 6150; **F:** 0131 455 6193
E: a.gray@napier.ac.uk; **W:** www.napier.ac.uk; www.publishingdegree.co.uk
MSc Publishing; MSc Magazine Publishing (subject to validation)

UNIVERSITY OF STIRLING
Stirling Centre for International Publishing and Communication, Department of English Studies, Pathfoot Building, University of Stirling, Stirling FK9 4LA
T: 01786 467 505; **F:** 01786 466 210
E: claire.squires@stir.ac.uk; **W:** www.publishing.stir.ac.uk
MLitt in Publishing Studies; MSc in International Publishing Management

SCOTTISH LITERARY AND BOOK FESTIVALS
For a list of the main literary and book festivals, see www.booksfromscotland.com

SCOTTISH LITERARY AWARDS AND PRIZES
For a list of the main literary awards and prizes, see www.booksfromscotland.com

TRAINING
ALPSP
Publishing courses in London, Oxford and in-house for the academic and professional publishing market
T: 01865 247 776; **E:** training@alpsp.org; **W:** www.alpsp.org

PUBLISHING IRELAND (FORMERLY CLÉ)
Publishing courses in Dublin
Guinness Enterprise Centre, Taylor's Lane, Dublin 8
T: 00 353 (0)1 415 1210; **E:** info@publishingireland.com;
W: www.publishingireland.com

LITERATURETRAINING
literaturetraining acts a first stop shop for writers and literature professionals across the UK looking for information and advice that will help them to move forward professionally
Literaturetraining, PO Box 23595, Leith EH6 7YX
T: 0131 553 2210; **E:** info@literaturetraining.com;
W: www.literaturetraining.com

MARKETABILITY
Publishing-focused marketing and editorial courses
12 Sandy Lane, Teddington, Middlesex TW11 0DR
T/F: 020 8977 2741; **E**: tellmemore@marketability.info;
W: www. marketability.info

NELSON CROOM
Distance learning publishing courses
N307 Westminster Business Square, 1–45 Durham Street, London SE11 5JH
T: 0207 582 3309; **E**: info@nelsoncroom.co.uk; **W**: www.nelsoncroom.co.uk

PUBLISHING SCOTLAND
The biggest provider of short publishing-related courses in Scotland. Courses
in Edinburgh and in-house include editorial, marketing, design, digital and
tailored in-house courses.
Scottish Book Centre, 137 Dundee Street, Edinburgh EH11 1BG
T: 0131 228 6866; **E**: enquiries@publishingscotland.org;
W: www.publishingscotland.org

PUBLISHING TRAINING CENTRE
Publishing courses in London and in-house, and distance learning
The Publishing Training Centre at Book House, 45 East Hill, Wandsworth,
London SW18 2QZ
T: 0208 874 2718; **E**: publishing.training@bookhouse.co.uk;
W: www.train4publishing.co.uk

SOCIETY FOR EDITORS AND PROOFREADERS
Editing and proofreading courses for freelancers and in-house staff at various
locations including London, Bristol, York and Edinburgh
SfEP Training, Erico House, 93–99 Upper Richmond Road, Putney,
London SW15 2TG
T: 0208 785 5617; **E**: trainingenquiries@sfep.org.uk; **W**: www.sfep.org.uk

Glossary

A selection of commonly-used terms and abbreviations in publishing

AI Advance Information Sheet. Bibliographic, sales and marketing information that should be sent by the publisher to those involved in selling the book well ahead of publication.

airport edition a specially prepared export edition of a book sold in airport retail outlets, generally before the paperback edition.

assignation of copyright the legal transmission of the entire copyright in a work. Assignation of copyright must be in writing. See also **copyright** and **licence**.

back orders orders made that could not immediately be fulfilled eg temporarily out-of-stock.

backlist a publisher's list of books that are still or kept in print (newly published books are known as the **frontlist**).

bcc back cover copy. Promotional writing on the back cover of the book.

BIC Book Industry Communication is an independent organisation that promotes supply chain efficiency in all sectors of the book world through e-commerce and the application of standard processes, procedures and book classification codes: see www.bic.org.uk.

bindings Paperbacks are usually perfect bound or slot (notch or burst) bound. Hardbacks are generally sewn bound. Perfect (unsewn or cutback) binding: an adhesive binding style where the backs of gathered sections are cut off and the leaves are glued at the binding edge. The most economical form of binding. Slot (notch or burst) binding: another form of adhesive binding in which a series of slots (or notches or nicks) are cut into the spine. Stronger than perfect binding and cheaper than sewn binding. Sewn binding: the strongest but most expensive form of binding.

blad basic layout and design. Pre-publication sample of a book usually comprising covers and some sample text and images.

blurb promotional writing on the cover or inside of a book.

book formats (UK trimmed page height/ width in millimetres).
A format: 178 × 110 (eg mass market paperback).
B format: 196 × 120 (trade paperback).
C format: 216 × 138 (popular hardback size: also called Metric Demy Octavo).
Metric Crown Octavo: 186 × 123.
Metric Large Crown Octavo: 198 × 129.
Metric Royal Octavo: 234 × 156 (popular hardback size).
Metric Crown Quarto: 246 × 189.
Pinched Crown Quarto: up to 249 × 175 (popular academic book size).
Metric Demy Quarto: 276 × 219.
Metric Royal Quarto: 312 × 237.
A4: 297 × 210 mm.
A5: 210 × 148 mm.

CIP Cataloguing-in-Publication. The British Library's CIP Programme provides records of new and forthcoming books in advance of publication in the United Kingdom and Ireland, which are included in the British National Bibliography (BNB). See www. bl.uk.

co-edition a co-edition is one of two or more editions of the same book, published by different publishers in different countries in the same or different languages.

co-publication publication between two or more publishers, or a publisher and another body (eg a professional organisation or charity).

copy-editing editing of copy (eg manuscript) to correct and/or style it to the publisher's standards to prepare for publication.

copyright copyright is the right of ownership in certain original works including literary and dramatic works and the typographical arrangement of published editions. For a useful overview of copyright and moral rights in the UK, see the websites of the UK Intellectual Property Office (www.ipo.gov.uk) and the Society of Authors (www.societyofauthors.org). See also **assignation of copyright** and **licence**.

cover the outside of a paperback book. See also **hardback** and **jacket**.

digital publishing electronic delivery of content.

aggregator: an aggregator licenses the right to distribute electronic content from publishers or other content providers. Aggregators may convert content into downloadable format as well as hosting or delivering.

DAD: digital asset distributor eg Libre Digital (www.libredigital.com); Ingram Digital (www.ingramdigital.com).

DAR: digital asset recipients (eg Google, Amazon, some aggregators).

DAP: digital asset producer (eg a publisher who provides content).

DAM: digital asset management (eg a system for organisation, retrieval, security etc of digital assets).

DRM: digital rights management systems seek to protect content from unauthorised use eg piracy by means including encryption codes, passwords etc.

discount reduction on the publisher's recommended price of a book given to a retailer to encourage stocking of the book (up to 60% for trade books).

distributor a distributor generally handles orders from retailers and wholesalers (sometimes end consumers) on terms set by the publisher, holds all of the publisher's stock and invoices and collects payment on behalf of the publisher. They may also provide other services. Contrast **wholesaler**.

dpi dots per inch. A measure of printing resolutions typically 300 dpi or more for books.

DTP desk top publishing. Adobe's InDesign is now establishing itself as the industry standard though QuarkXPress is still widely used.

dues orders made on a book prior to publication. Often used by a publisher to decide on the size of the **print run**. See also **subscriptions**.

ebook electronic book. Many books are now available as ebooks to be read on screens including smart phones and portable ebook readers. There is no standard ebook format: PDFs display well on computers but not on smaller portable devices and some proprietary ebook formats are readable on only one brand of ereader (though most ereaders can read more than one format of ebook).

EDI electronic data interchange.

edition the version eg first, second, third etc. A new edition is generally the result of significant changes. If only minor changes are required, a **reprint** rather than a new edition may be published.

emarketing marketing using the internet eg e-alerts, RSS feeds, website promotions, **SEO** etc.

end matter material that appears at the end of a book after the main text eg appendix, bibliography, index, references.

EPOS electronic point of sale systems are used to record sales or other transactions between retailers and customers.

EPS See *Image file formats*.

ereader a portable device for reading digital print (commonly ebooks but also newspapers, magazines, comics etc).

extent the number of pages or words in a book.

fee the payment (usually a one-off) made to an author instead of a **royalty**. Common in certain types of publishing eg academic and professional.

frontlist a publisher's newly published books (previous publications still or kept in print are known as the **backlist**).

gsm grams per square metre. The measure of paper weight used in printing: heavier for art books, lighter for paperbacks.

hardback (hardcover) a book with rigid covers.

house style a consistent style particular to a company, publication etc. For an example, see the online version of the *Guardian Style Guide* (www.guardian.co.uk/styleguide).

HTML Hypertext Markup Language is the predominant language used to create web pages.

Image file formats
For print:
EPS: encapsulated PostScript.
TIFF: tagged image file format.
For website:
GIF: graphics interchange format (an older format suitable for small website images).
JPEG: joint photographic experts group (best for photographic images).
PNG: portable network graphics (a modern replacement for GIF).

Imprint a brand name for a list of books at a publisher. A publisher may have several imprints eg Waverley Books is an imprint of Geddes & Grosset.

IPR intellectual property rights (the main IPRs are copyright, designs, patents and trademarks). The UK Intellectual Property Office (Patent Office) website contains useful information (www.ipo.gov.uk).

ISBN International Standard Book Number. An ISBN is a unique 13-digit product number used by publishers, libraries, distributors, retailers etc for listing and stock control purposes. The ISBN Agency is the national agency for the UK and Republic of Ireland: see www.isbn.nielsenbookdata.co.uk.

ISSN the ISSN (International Standard Serial Number) is an 8-digit number which identifies periodical publications as such, including electronic serials: see www.issn.org

jacket the detachable dust jacket protecting a hardcover book.

JPEG see *Image file formats*.

legal deposit designated libraries or archives (which include the National Library of Scotland, Edinburgh), are legally entitled to request a copy of all printed items published in the United Kingdom, and in the Republic of Ireland by reciprocal legislation. They can also request the deposit of some categories of non-print material. For further information, see www.nls.uk/about/legaldeposit.

licence a licence is a permission that allows a publisher to publish copyrighted work. Under a licence the publisher does not acquire the entire copyright (compare **assignation of copyright**). An exclusive licence (which must be in writing) means that the publisher has a right to publish that excludes all others including the copyright owner; a non-exclusive licence allows for similar licences to be granted to others. The terms of the licence determine the rights granted eg sub-licensing, publication and distribution, formats, languages, territories and duration.

literal see **typo**

Long Tail The theory of the Long Tail is that due to the proliferation and freedom of choice, there is a move away from a focus on 'hits' (the most popular products and markets at the 'head' of the demand curve) towards a huge number of non-hits in the 'tail' of the demand curve. So for a publisher the Long Tail theory may mean it is profitable to publish **POD** copies of lots of less popular but steadily-selling books in the backlist that they might previously have allowed to go out of print. For more information, see Chris Anderson's blog: www.thelongtail.com.

manuscript the text from the author (originally handwritten but now a typescript). Abbreviated to MS (plural MSS).

moral rights moral rights are concerned with protecting the personality and reputation of authors. They include the right to be identified as author of the work (where that right has been asserted), the right to object to derogatory treatment of the work and the right not to have work falsely attributed to the author. For a useful overview of copyright and moral rights in the UK, see the websites of the UK Intellectual Property Office (www.ipo.gov.uk) and the Society of Authors (www.societyofauthors.org).

NBA the Net Book Agreement was an arrangement between publishers and retailers that books would be sold at a set price without discounts to the consumer. It was abandoned in 1995/1996 and was ruled illegal in 1997.

net receipts/net sales revenue (NSR) receipts of revenue after deduction of discount. Royalties are generally based on net receipts.

on-screen editing copy-editing on screen using macros, stylesheets etc.

ONIX promoted by **BIC** as the international standard, ONIX is a standard means by which product data can be transmitted electronically by publishers to data aggregators, wholesalers, booksellers and anyone else involved in the sale of their publications: see www.editeur.org

OP/Out of print no longer in print. Many formerly 'out of print' books have been revived by their original or other publishers aided by *POD, Project Gutenberg* etc.

packager a company that produces (or is commissioned to produce) a finished book which is then sold by a publisher.

paperback a book with paper covers.

PDF portable document format: an electronic document standard used for print, web and ebooks. An extension of **EPS**.

POD print on demand. Developments in print technology now allow economical and good quality print on demand of single books or short runs of books. Providers range from traditional printers to some booksellers using small printing presses such as The Espresso Book Machine (EBM).

podcast an audio or video file that is published on the internet for downloading.

POS material point of sale material is material produced by publishers to promote titles in a retail environment.

preliminary pages preliminary pages (or prelim pages, prelims) are pages at the beginning of a book before the text. Preliminary pages commonly comprise some or all of the following: title, half-title, imprint page, contents, preface, foreword.

print run the number of copies of a book printed at one time. A print run can range from a short run with fewer than 500 to millions for bestsellers such as the *Harry Potter* books.

printing printing is the business of a printer.

Project Gutenberg the first and largest single collection of free electronic books or eBooks set up by Michael Hart to encourage the creation and distribution of eBooks (www.gutenberg.org).

proofreading the checking of the proof copy by comparison with the typescript and/or by reading straight through.

proposal a written presentation of a potential publication (eg to a literary agent, publisher, publications board). Elements vary between fiction and non-fiction but commonly include: overview, market, competing titles, outline, list of contents, sample chapter, author biography.

Publishing 'Publishing *n* the business of producing and offering for sale books, newspapers etc' - *The Chambers Dictionary* (11th edn, 2008). Publishing is a complex business that involves selecting content, scheduling, editing, design, production, marketing, sales, distribution, finance and rights management.

puff praise for a book that appears on a book cover (current trend is to seek puffs from well-known authors, celebrities etc).

recto a right-hand page.

reprint when a **print run** is depleted and there is evidence that demand for a book is high, the publisher will order a reprint. Contrast **edition**.

returns unsold books that are returned by the retailer to the publisher.

royalty a contractual payment made to an author calculated on the number of copies sold or a percentage of the sales income. Royalty percentages vary and may be based on the **net sales revenue** or the price of the book. See also **fee**.

RSS really simple syndication is a type of web feed format that allows regular new or updated content to be distributed to subscribers (eg Canongate Books' RSS feeds for Meet at the Gate news: www.canongate.net).

running head a headline at the very top of a page: commonly a chapter title, other main hierarchical heading (in academic or professional books or encyclopaedias) or word (in dictionaries).

self-publishing publishing organised and paid for by the author of the work. The Society of Authors produces a *Quick Guide to Self Publishing and Print on Demand* as well as useful advice on its website: see www.societyofauthors.org. Not to be confused with **vanity publishing**.

SEO search engine optimization, ie the process of making a website rank high in major search engines when a specific word or phrase is searched.

serial rights the right to reproduce parts of a book before its publication (first serial rights) or after its publication (second serial rights) over a period of time (eg daily or weekly extracts in a newspaper, magazine or digital medium).

site licence a licence that allows multiple users at a site (or multiple sites) to access online material or software.

SOR sale or return. See **returns**.

spine the backbone of a book. In the UK the title is usually written from top to bottom.

Subscriptions (or subs) orders for books received in advance of publication. See also **dues**.

subsidiary rights rights other than **volume rights**. Subsidiary rights include eg first, second and subsequent serial rights; audio rights; film, documentary and dramatisation rights; and translation rights.

TPS trimmed page size.

trade publishing the type of publishing (eg fiction, general non-fiction and reference) that is sold mainly through book trade and other retailers to consumers. Other types of publishing include: academic (higher education), schools, STM (scientific, technical and medical), and professional (eg accountancy, law, tax). Non-trade publishing is generally sold through specialist channels.

typo (or literal) a typographic error in printed material resulting from a mistake made when keying or setting text.

USP unique selling proposition or unique selling point: originally the specific benefits of a product that the competition does not or cannot offer. More realistically in publishing is that the USP defines what will make a book sell.

VAT value added tax is a UK tax on goods and services payable by the seller to the government. Printed books are zero-rated for VAT but it is currently charged at standard rate on digital products including audiobooks, ebooks, videos and DVDs. The standard rate of VAT was temporarily reduced to 15% on 1 December 2008 and returned to 17.5% on 1 January 2010. EU proposals for reduced rate VAT on audio books have not yet been implemented.

vanity publishing vanity publishing is a service whereby authors pay to have their work published by a publisher who purports to offer traditional publishing services (eg selection, editing, marketing and sales) but in practice does not provide these services. Eg a vanity publisher will publish the work of anyone who pays. A vanity publisher derives profit solely from money paid by the author and returns little or nothing to the author through sales of books or rights. Contrast with **self publishing**.

verso a left-hand page.

viral marketing marketing that relies on customers and prospects to spread the message through social networking.

visual (or mock-up) a layout or rough of a cover or jacket design.

volume rights basic publishing rights permitting publication of a book in hardcover and paperback formats in English for the UK market. See also **subsidiary rights**.

wasting unsold overstock, damaged returns etc that cannot be sold may be disposed of by shredding or other method of destruction.

Web 2.0 a catch-all term for a variety of website technologies and processes which facilitate user interaction, user-generated content (eg Wikipedia and YouTube), and web-based applications such as Gmail and Zoho Office.

wholesaler a wholesaler buys in stock from many publishers and sells to retailers.

widget a mini-application that allows content to be added to blogs, web pages

etc: eg a widget to provide the display of the current number of visitors online at a website.

WOM word of mouth: the form of recommendation most trusted by readers. See also **viral marketing**.

XML Extensible Markup Language is a method of tagging text according to a Document Type Definition (DTD) and facilitates single-sourcing of material for publication in formats other than print.

Index